DECEIVED

by

BRENDA BURLING

CRANTHORPE
MILLNER

First published by Cranthorpe Millner Publishers (2021)

ISBN 978-1-912964-59-8 (Paperback)

www.cranthorpemillner.com

Cranthorpe Millner Publishers

For My Boys

Acknowledgements

Endless thanks and appreciation to Lady 'L' for her tireless encouragement, support, lightning fingers and continuous rallying of my cause. Further thanks to Fay and Doodle for their expert navigation of all matters alien to me – I would still be lost without you.

To all family and friends, without whom I may never have attempted this maiden voyage.

With unlimited appreciation to 'D' who in his own way made absolutely sure I achieved my goal, "if only to wipe the smile off old Puddy Arms' face".

Without love there is nothing.

1.

The school run always made me tense. Today was particularly bad; the pouring rain had started the previous afternoon and showed no sign of slowing. I thought it wise I left a little earlier than normal to make the usual thirty-five-minute drive. Unfortunately, the rest of Cambridge's commuter community had the same idea. Having turned onto Trumpington Road towards the school, the traffic came to a standstill.

At last, having dropped the children off at school, I went on to indulge my much-loved habit of shopping. I revelled in Cambridge's hidden boutiques, where a one-off treasure could still be found. A brief, yet fruitful, trip now resulted in the seats of my Mercedes being piled high with the likes of Prada, Gucci, and Chanel, as well as one or two lesser known yet equally talented designers. All the wrappings now converged together in a kaleidoscope of colour against the cream leather upholstery of the back seat of my car.

Two thousand pounds spent in a matter of hours; a paltry sum and hardly worth a mention at tonight's dinner table. My much-loved midnight blue C220 swiftly responded to the pressure from my foot on the accelerator. As my foot pressed down, a little slippery on the pedal due to the rain, I admired my gold sandals. They were particularly striking coupled with my latest pedicure – though what I was thinking with my choice of footwear this morning was anyone's guess. Hunter wellies would have been more appropriate but alas, hardly went with the outfit of the day.

When I first saw the shoes, I had that stomach aching need, reminiscent of childhood in its intensity. The same all-consuming need experienced when you meet the man you know will become your husband. or when your newborn baby looks up at you for the first time. That need had become a part of everyday life for me, satisfied through shopping; it was my addiction. I chose to view my shopping as an art form and my numerous custom-made wardrobes, my gallery. My husband, Mike, didn't always share my vision, having given up long ago trying to understand my passion for fashion and all things beautiful.

Luckily, I knew of a couple of secret little parking bays in the middle of town, close to King's College and my favourite shops. Most people never took the chance of getting stuck down a tiny street with a parking warden merrily tapping away on their ticket machine, whilst you tried to talk your way out of a ticket without running them over.

I checked my watch whilst sitting in the still-heavy traffic, thinking now was a respectable time to call Marcia. The car's on-board phone system was voice-activated, and I always felt rather ridiculous talking out loud to piece of machinery.

"Marcia's home number," I said loudly. A moment's pause and an automated voice filled the car.

"Unable to connect your call. Please contact your network provider."

"Why can I never get these blasted gadgets to work first time?" Cursing in frustration, I tried again, this time mouthing the words with deliberate emphasis. "Marcia's home number," I shouted, incapable of hiding my irritation.

The same automated response came back instantly. I sighed. Maybe I was in a bad reception area. There was still a fair amount of traffic on the roads, even for this time of day; I figured it must be due to the bad weather. I decided to pull over at the next convenient place instead of trying to traverse the overflowing drains and dozens of students on bikes, all sporting a muddy stripe up their backs from the combination of unguarded rear wheels and wet, dirty roads.

The lay-by I had in mind came into view and I pulled over without too much fuss. There was no hurry; after all I had no job and no beauty appointments in my diary today. Calming down a little, I made an effort to gather my thoughts and relax. Checking my make-up in the interior rear-view mirror, I was pleasantly surprised to see all was as it should be, which wasn't bad considering the rain.

I tried the phone again, and again, the reply was the same. "Christ, why does this happen to me?" I shouted to nobody. "Bloody technology. Would be quicker to use a call box." *Must stop talking to myself*, I reprimanded.

The heat was increasing in the car; even though there was rain, it was still humid and I was grateful when the icy blast emitted from the air vents with the start of the engine. Cool beads of sweat had gathered on my top lip, which made me curse loudly – my make-up would need retouching after all. In fact, a shower when I got home wouldn't go amiss.

I needed to get home. Irritation was getting the better of me; with a heavy foot, I accelerated along Trumpington Road heading home. The traffic thinned substantially as I turned off onto the B1356, and, remembering the continuous twisting and turning of the winding country road I was now on, I eased off the gas and forced my mind to calm. .

The final turn off into the village of Havington was on a sharp bend, which if you weren't in the know, could quite easily have you sitting in the middle of the ditch running along both sides of the road. Once, not long after we moved in, Mike had found himself in the ditch when he hadn't been fully concentrating on driving home from work.

We had fallen in love with the place about the same time Mike and I had first started going out together. We found ourselves lost one rainy Sunday afternoon and had sought refuge in the pub; the village itself consisted of that one pub, a tiny shop which doubled as a post office and a beautiful duck pond. It was almost untouched by the modern world and was always a haven to come home to.

As the chimneys of *Finetrees* came into view, I smiled to myself. I never tired of spotting the three sets of red brick pillars topped with ornate chimney pots which signified home. I was proud of my home and would admit we lived a blessed life. The hardships of the past when we first married were not completely forgotten however – I remembered having to crouch behind the front door, knowingly avoiding the landlord as the rent was late, again. Thankfully, that period of poverty was short-lived and we could now look back on it with some humour.

As a family, we now enjoyed the best that life had to offer. Pulling onto our drive, I cast my mind back. It wasn't long after Mike and I married that we discovered we were expecting twin girls. They were summer babies. Naming them Alice and Phoebe, we chose a private school and reserved their places immediately. From then, we hired a nanny, cook, gardener and various other cleaners; the only task I undertook was the daily school run as our nanny, Agnes, didn't drive.

As new parents, we wanted our children to have the best start in life and consequently, they were a little spoilt but not rude or boastful. From an early age, I tried to instil in them the need to be kind and gracious wherever possible, and for them to try to remember other people's feelings.

Alice was the more sensitive of the two, taking almost everything to heart and worrying over the slightest thing. Phoebe, on the other hand, had the stronger personality and had taken on the role of protector as soon as she could walk, standing up for her sister whether she needed to or not. She was also more argumentative and slightly prone to mood swings.

However, they both shared a quirky sense of humour, finding the oddest things hilarious and, like a lot of twins, had long perfected the art of finishing each other's sentences, which could be as equally annoying as endearing.

As they grew older, the girls bore a striking resemblance to myself, both being auburn haired with a fair complexion and small stature, though they had their father's eyes, cornflower blue. Most days when I collected Alice and Phoebe from school, we would go into Cambridge to have a quick look around the shops and have coffee, rarely returning home empty handed. I loved to shop with them. In fact, spending any time at all with them made me happy; our connection was so intense that I missed them when they were at school and most days, I would be waiting around eagerly for school pick-up time.

***

As the drive opened out into the courtyard area at the front of the house, I abandoned the car just outside the front door and let myself into the cool hallway. I called out for Daphne, our cook-cum-housekeeper who had become a permanent member of the family since the birth of our children. Usually at this time of day, she would be ensconced in the kitchen making cakes or cookies.

"Daphne, I'm back, sorry I missed you earlier." Having left early that morning, guessing that traffic would be bad due to the weather, I had been gone before the staff started their day. There was no reply, so I called out again; Daphne was almost seventy and her hearing was failing her. I made my way to the kitchen and pushed the swinging door open gently – having done it with some force on a previous occasion, sending Daphne, complete with a substantial number of teacakes, tumbling to the floor.

It was obvious she wasn't about, nor had been at all that day; the highly polished, spotlessly clean chrome kitchen gleamed silently back at me. There wasn't a single thing out of place. Although puzzled, I wasn't overly concerned. Mike may have given her a day off and failed to mention it. In fact, thinking about it, he may have told me before he left at 5am that morning, but I'd have been barely conscious. I'd long perfected the art of grunting in the right places, even when asleep, to make it sound like I was listening to everything he had to say.

I'd been concerned for some time that the hours Mike worked were increasing at an alarming rate; he was barely home and I'd been meaning to bring it up for discussion with him, but like most other matters that weren't to do with shopping or our children, I'd never gotten around to it.

Leaving the kitchen, I went back into the hallway to use the phone, having finally found my diary amidst so much other paraphernalia I deemed necessary to be carted around in my oversized Prada bag. Flicking through to M in the address section, I found the mobile phone company's number. The house phone was to be avoided whenever possible; a huge, mock old-fashioned porcelain contraption Mike had bought because he thought it would be 'fun'. Not so much fun when you're trying to balance it between your ear and shoulder.

I had just about balanced it perfectly and was about to start dialling when I noticed there was no dialling tone – there was no sound at all. Frantically, I began depressing the receiver cradle, though why I expected this to make a difference, I don't know. It didn't. Now unnerved, I was increasingly aware the house was silent; there was no noise from the garden either.

Mr Green, the gardener, came every day to perform one miracle or another on the acres of lawn, flowerbeds, orchard and water gardens that made up the grounds of the house. There was usually the hum of the ride-on lawn mower in the distance, or sometimes the louder grating of the chainsaw if he was sawing logs for the fire. Always, the muffled sound of the radio drifted from one of the greenhouses, but today, there was nothing.

Running through the house, I called for the people I normally spent my days with, but no answer came. Panic rose, accompanied by acid-tasting bile, as I took the stairs to the upper floor two at a time. Agnes, our nanny, or 'super nanny' as the children liked to call her, would normally be straightening out the chaos always left in their wake. Running from one room to the next, it was obvious there was no sign of her. The girl's room remained untouched by Agnes' miraculous efficiency. A collection of CDs, clothes and brightly coloured hair accessories were scattered to the four corners of the room.

A cold prickliness of fear crashed over me in waves. I was beginning to feel I was stuck in a nightmare; the scene was normal, except all human participation had been completely erased. There was nobody to talk to within the house and no way of contacting anybody outside of it.

Running back downstairs, I grabbed my bag and keys from the table and fled. Once outside, I found the sun had broken through the clouds and the rain had stopped, a gentle warmth filling the air. I tried to take some comfort from it and rationalise the situation.

Could it be a simple case of Mike having given the staff some time off? He did consider it his responsibility to take care of domestic arrangements, particularly the staffing. I'd been involved with the selection of the nanny, but only because I had insisted and made a fuss until Mike finally relented.

2.

I needed to see Marcia, my oldest and closest friend. Marcia also enjoyed a privileged lifestyle, though hers was accentuated by her own family background; her family had been influential in commercial investments for the last two hundred years and had been involved in funding some of the world's most famous building projects. She was 'old money' wealthy.

As a child, she had summered in the South of France aboard the family yacht and spent time with family and friends in places such as Rome, Paris and New York. These were all considered normal pastimes for her, along with a private education, clothes allowance and a hefty inheritance being staple components of her upbringing.

Marcia's husband, Alex, was Mike's business partner and, like Mike, was a self-made man. Together, they had built an engineering company from scratch, providing engine components to the motor manufacturing industry. They had become one of the leading companies in the country and were now preparing to go global.

By the time I reached her house, a million different scenarios had played themselves out in my mind. After a few moments of frantic, harsh knocking, Marcia opened the door. Judging by the worried look on her face when she saw me, she could tell something was wrong.

"Julia, what on earth has happened?" she cried, ushering me inside.

I tried to convey the morning's events, but it came out in an incoherent ramble; even to myself, the words I spoke sounded unbelievable. I was beginning to feel a little foolish in front of my friend, who lived a rather ordered and undramatic life. Marcia gently led me to the drawing room and rang for some coffee.

By the time coffee had arrived, I had calmed down a little and was able to properly describe what had happened. Marcia listened demurely, her perfectly shaped eyebrow raised quizzically.

"Darling, Mike probably just gave the staff time off, as you say." She looked thoughtful as she sipped her coffee and added, "And as for your phone, you know we've had some terrible weather recently, our phone lines were brought down only the other week, do you remember? It took two whole days to get things rectified. I think you're putting two and two together and coming up with five," she laughed gently, pleased with her little joke.

I thought for a moment. She was probably right, as usual. I'd always thought of Marcia as one of life's calm people; she was rarely unnerved or agitated by anything, never in an obvious hurry and yet, never late.

"Why not call the phone company now and find out what's going on?" added Marcia. "If it's their fault, you can give them hell. If it's something Mike has organised and not told you, you can give him hell later tonight," she finished, obviously satisfied with her reasoning. "Getting upset like this isn't going to solve anything."

"I'm sorry, Marci, I'm sure you're right and I'm just overreacting. I'll go call them now and then take you to Andre's for lunch, as a thank you. What would I do without you?" I forced a smile as I left to go to the hall.

"Darling, it's what I'm here for, but you know me – I never say no to lunch at Andre's! I'll just go and change."

The beautifully tailored cream suit Marcia wore was wrinkle free, but I knew my friend wouldn't dream of attending lunch in an outfit she had worn in the morning. I watched as she glided past me out of the room with barely a sound, reprimanding myself silently for being so melodramatic.

Having located my diary for the second time that morning, I dialled the phone company again. There was barely a single ring before the call was answered.

"Good morning, can I help you?" The customer service advisor had an unfortunate nasal drawl that gave an impression of terminal boredom.

"I hope so. It would appear my mobile isn't working. I can't make any outgoing calls." I tried to sound as reasonable as possible.

"I see, is there a particular response when you try to use your phone?" She now sounded irritated, as well as bored.

"It's along the lines of 'it's not possible to connect your call, please contact your network provider,' or something like that." I knew I was beginning to sound a little curt but couldn't quite help myself.

The operator's tone changed and sounded triumphant with her reply. "Well, madam, that's the usual response when the phone company has disconnected the service."

"Can you tell me why you would do that?" I asked, desperately trying to keep my cool whilst a prickly sensation of panic made the hairs on the back of my neck stand up.

"Madam, we at Fonemax reserve the right to cancel the contract for any number of reasons." The smug tone of her reply made my blood boil, but I knew I had to keep calm and sound as pleasant as possible to get the answers I needed.

"Could you possibly check your records and see if there's anything there that might suggest a reason for my phone not working?" I waited for the reply. The line went silent for a moment followed by dreadful hold music. Another moment passed, and she was back on the line.

"Madam, there's no new phone on order and your phone has been disconnected due to non-payment of invoices."

"Non-payment of invoices!" I barked, all self-control gone. "Have you any idea how ridiculous that is? It must be a mistake."

"No madam, I've double checked and it's not just the one invoice that remains unpaid; the last three are outstanding."

I was dumbstruck. Mike paid all the bills, there were never any problems – how could this have happened? Realising there was no point continuing the conversation, I ended the call.

I stood still in the grand hallway; I wasn't sure what to do next. I paused, making up my mind, before dialling the number for the landline provider. I had a bad feeling about speaking to them too; a moment later, my fears were confirmed. The company said they had received a letter from Mike, explaining that as of the eleventh of the month, the landline would no longer be required as the property had been sold. I dropped the receiver in complete shock.

My mind was a grey fog; today was the eleventh. I felt Marcia's presence as she stood quietly behind me. "Something's very wrong. My mobile's been cut off because of unpaid bills. And it gets worse, the landline has also been disconnected. Apparently, Mike wrote to the supplier to advise them that the house has been sold and the service will not be required as of the eleventh of the month."

It was clear that Marcia didn't know what to say or do. A split-second later, a look flashed across her face: embarrassment. My best friend of countless years, someone with whom I had shared a million thoughts and feelings with, was embarrassed – whether for me, or by me, I couldn't tell. I felt abandoned.

Marcia opened her mouth once or twice as if to say something but gave up. I went into the drawing room, picked up my coat, turned and headed back to the hallway towards the front door. As I turned the handle, a hand came to rest on my shoulder.

"Let's go to Andre's and we'll call Mike at the office. We can take my car," Marcia suggested softly.

I was grateful for both the offer and the company, feeling I needed someone with me when I spoke to Mike. Easing myself into the passenger seat of the Bentley, I replayed in my mind the bizarre string of events that had taken place. I managed to talk myself into a dozen different plausible explanations.

It was possible the unpaid bills could have been the result of a disagreement Mike had with the phone company and him wanting to teach them a lesson by not paying. It was also possible that the house phone disconnected because he had found a better deal elsewhere and had written to say the house had been sold to avoid cancellation costs.

Neither scenario felt right to me, even as I prayed they were.

3.

With a sense of deep foreboding, I realised I had no idea what was or had been going on recently, and the individual incidents culminated into one definitive conclusion: I'd been kept in the dark about an awful lot. Thinking about Mike and our relationship, I realised we hadn't conducted a decent conversation in weeks, and hadn't been intimate in what must have been months. It was easy to claim distraction with the children around but I knew this wasn't the real reason, though I felt incapable of defining the actual cause of our relationship breakdown. Mike had been spending huge amounts of time at the office and I had made a promise to myself I would try and talk to him about it, not that it had ever happened. It suddenly hit me; we had become strangers over the last couple of months.

"Think you should give the office a call?" Marcia's voice broke into my thoughts.

"I suppose I should really. Maybe a few words from him and the whole morning can be put down to early onset menopause. Either way, there must be a logical explanation," I replied brightly. My voice sounded more confident than I felt; I was desperately trying to be positive.

Marcia, having been driving steadily towards Cambridge city centre, had now pulled over and spoke the command for her phone to dial the company's offices. I readied myself, feeling the need to speak extra clear. I still felt that maybe, somehow, this situation might be my own doing. The receptionist answered almost immediately.

"Hello Clare, Julia Weston here. Is Mr Weston available please?"

There was a pause. "But Mrs Weston, Mr Weston is away on business for two weeks, I thought you knew?"

My heart froze. My throat tightened, as if there were a noose wrapped around it, and I could taste bile rising. Almost unable to speak, I realised the young girl on the other end of the line was waiting, as was Marcia. With effort, and with courage I didn't truly feel, I spoke.

"Of course, Clare, what am I thinking of? I'll call him on his mobile." Just as I was about to end the call, Marcia spoke.

"Hi, Clare, Marcia Claremont here. Could you pass me through to my husband please?"

"Of course, Mrs Claremont, please hold a moment."

Two clicks and then the ringing tone of Alex's extension was heard. He picked up on the third ring.

"Alex, it's me. Just a quick one – is Mike in the office today?"

"No darling, Mike's in New York on business. It was pretty last-minute. Anything wrong?"

"No, not a problem, Julia just has a fault with her phone. We're off to Andre's now for lunch. I'm sure Julia must have forgotten about the trip; you know how she is ... so busy all the time. Take care my love, see you tonight. Love you. Bye." Marcia ended the call.

"Thanks Marci, for playing things down. I feel like I'm losing my mind – why would he keep a business trip from me?" I was staring out at the fields through the car window, my mind trying to run over anything that might have been said. Something, anything, I might have missed, or hadn't given my full attention to at the time. I was unable to come up with any answers. Marcia had no answers and made no attempt to give any.

"All I do know, is that you're going to drive yourself insane if you don't speak to Mike soon," she offered at last.

"I'll give his mobile another call." I knew my tone had a touch of hysteria and I prayed for the call to be picked up. Instead, my call simply rang out again. My hands now shaking, the feeling of nausea was overpowering. Throwing open the car door, I vomited. Marcia looked at me in disbelief.

"Dear God, Julia, I'm taking you home. You can't let people see you like this."

"Yes, take me home, Marci, please, just take me home," I sobbed, roughly wiping my face with my sleeve.

We drove back to *Finetrees* in silence while I continued trying Mike's mobile number. Marcia took the phone and, with her leading me by the arm, I managed to let us in before slumping into an armchair in the sitting room. I could see from the expression on Marcia's face she was concerned for me. I still felt like I was being choked, barely able to get my breath. I hoped I wasn't having some sort of breakdown.

Marcia found some brandy and poured a huge measure, handing me the glass and making sure I had it in both hands. I drank it in one. It made me grimace and splutter, though there was comfort in the burning liquid as it forced my limbs to relax slightly.

"Now, calm down and think. Are you absolutely sure Mike never mentioned anything to you about the house, the trip or any of this?"

I almost laughed out loud at the absurdity of the question. "Well, of course he didn't," I said, my exasperation clearly evident.

Marcia offered to make coffee which caused me to smile; I wasn't even sure she knew how. Clearly she needed a distraction whilst I continued to try Mike's number.

"Any luck?" Marcia asked, as she passed me a cup on her return.

"No, it just rings out to voicemail. I can leave a message, but what do I say? Where are you, why do I have no phone? Why am I being told my house has been sold and where the hell have all the staff gone?" Tears were stinging my eyes. My hysteria was rising again and I knew I sounded a little unhinged.

Tired and dejected, I rose to go to the bathroom to freshen up. I needed time to myself, to think. As I passed Marcia, she gently touched my arm and offered a weak smile of reassurance that only just shone through the pained look that now shadowed her face. I took Marcia's mobile phone with me, and as if on autopilot, pressed the redial button every few minutes.

4.

The bathroom adjoining the master bedroom had always been my favourite place to relax; it was my sanctuary. There was nothing I loved more than adding a few drops of bath oil to scalding hot water and luxuriating in the bubbles, soaking away the stresses of the day. The room, with its soft, subtle, slightly pink down lighting and warm ochre tones, never failed to calm me. Today, however, as I stared into the mirror, I looked and felt wretched.

I liked to think of myself as a modest person, but I didn't mind occasionally admitting that on a good day I looked a little younger than my years. My complexion was light, and I had freckles which I'd hated until my late twenties, at which point I realised they were probably what gave me a youthful edge. Normally, I tried to make the best of my appearance, but I wasn't in the mood; my face, now devoid of make-up due to crying, was wan and puffy, and I had no intention of wasting time to rectify it.

The cool water felt good as I cupped my hands under the running tap and splashed my face. I said a silent prayer, hoping I was, in fact, dreaming and thought now would be as good a time as any to wake up from the nightmare. The prayer remained unanswered.

As I patted my face dry and turned to replace the towel on the warming rail, I pressed the redial button again on the mobile phone.

From the corner of my eye, I suddenly became aware of something so fleeting that I wasn't sure I'd seen anything at all. Turning my face and pressing the redial button again, this time I was sure; a pale green glow on the bedside cabinet, visible only for a moment before it was gone again. I knew what it was before I'd even reached Mike's side of the bed.

Mike's mobile lay on its side. Being a slimline model, I hadn't noticed it there. If I was being honest, I was never particularly interested in what Mike had on his bedside table; he was hardly the harbinger of articles of great interest or night-time reading. I picked up the black and silver Android phone and turned it over in my hand to see the display. The bright green backlight shone again, illuminating the screen display – and the 23 missed calls. I might as well have been slapped in the face – every time Marcia or I had called Mike's phone, it had registered the call unanswered.

A wave of anxiety engulfed me once more. I wanted to scream, cry and destroy anything within my grasp, but the energy with which to do that eluded me. I felt beaten. Phone in hand, I left the bedroom and returned to Marcia, handing her the phone before sitting down heavily. Silently, I drank the lukewarm, bitter tasting coffee. A black veil of depression hung over me as I morosely stared at the phone in my friend's hand.

I don't know how long we sat in absolute silence; Marcia not uttering a word and barely making a sound as she breathed. I felt she was unwittingly rooted to the spot, unable to make the decision to move, the tension in the room so great. Slowly in my mind, matters and events began to shift themselves into order. A spark of clarity inspired and awakened my sense of survival; there were actions that needed to be taken. Instinct told me there'd be more of this nightmare to come, but I had to deal with the here and now. I had to speak to Mike, even though I knew that wasn't going to be easy.

Not saying a word, I took Mike's phone from Marcia, who still had it in the palm of her hand as if it may bite her should she move. I dialled the Claremont and Weston office once more, snorting derisively at the irony of Mike's phone remaining unaffected and working perfectly. Clare answered again.

"Hello Clare, it's Mrs Weston again. I wonder, could you tell me what the flight number was for my husband's trip to New York? Oh, and Clare, could I have the telephone number of his hotel? He did give it to me, but I seem to have lost it." Mind sparking, I quickly added, "Just one more thing while you're on, could you let me have the phone number of his client in New York? He likes me to have a number in case of emergencies." The line went silent whilst she went to retrieve the information.

I allowed myself a concealed half-smile as I glanced across at Marcia, whose gaped mouth was opening and closing soundlessly like a fish out of water. Her eyes were huge saucer-like shapes of disbelief at my pretence. I guessed, from the ever so slightly furrowed brow and pained expression on her face, that the course of the morning's events had completely wiped her out.

Unimaginably, I felt a new feeling of strength spreading through me. My sense of survival engulfed me, and my mind seemed slightly clearer. Feeling concerned, I was about to ask her if she was feeling all right when Clare came back on the line, and I returned my focus to the conversation.

"Hello, Mrs Weston?"

"Yes, I'm still here, Clare."

"I'm sorry, Mrs Weston, Mr Weston made all his own arrangements as the trip was a last-minute rush. He didn't leave any details," she continued in a tone of apologetic embarrassment, as if somehow it was her fault. "As for the client he intended to meet, Mr Claremont may have their number, but I don't appear to have that either."

"Thanks for your help, Clare. I wonder if you could put me through to Mr Claremont?"

"Certainly, please hold for a moment."

For the second time, the line went silent. Suddenly, the booming voice of Alex Claremont came on the line.

"Hello Julia, how's things?"

"Not so good actually, Alex." I had lost the will to try and pretend all was well, when it quite obviously wasn't. "My telephone at home is disconnected, I appear to have no staff and according to one source, my home has been sold. Oh, and to top it all off, I can't get a hold of Mike. His mobile is here, and he's left no details as to his whereabouts."

"Well, that's easy – he's gone to see the American branch of the Nagosaki Corporation. As for his travel itinerary, I'm afraid I don't have that, but if I give you the client's number, you can at least leave a message for him." The soothing tone and certainty in Alex's voice gave no indication of anything being amiss, and I began to feel slightly neurotic.

"Thanks very much, Alex. I'm sorry to have interrupted you but this morning has left me slightly unnerved," I said truthfully.

"I'm sure there's nothing to worry about, and as soon as you speak to Mike everything will be sorted out. Now then, that number, where did I put it?" There was the sound of paper shuffling. "Here it is. The number is 555-479-2314 and I believe he is seeing Mr Simco."

"Thanks again, Alex. Would you like to speak to Marci?"

A denial from Alex was heard, so I clicked off the call, thanking him one more time, then I immediately dialled the New York number. Unfortunately, due to the time difference, there was only security answering. Looking at my watch and noticing it was lunchtime, I knew I should have some lunch but didn't feel I'd be able to eat anything. I also had a compelling urge to be alone.

Fortunately, Marcia was only too pleased to be excused from the situation. It was obvious she felt matters had taken a sordid turn and she was out of her comfort zone. If this nightmare, which had become my day, was just made up of a series of coincidences and misunderstandings, that was all well and good, but I had my doubts.

I watched from the front door as Marcia eased herself into her car. Even from where I stood, I could see her shoulders relax as the tension left her body. She turned the car slowly in the courtyard to face the way we had come in and wound down the window, waving farewell. We made promises to call each other and confirmed arrangements for one of her staff to drop my car off to me later that day.

I turned back into the silence of my home. Standing motionless, I tried to absorb and, once again, make sense of the day's events, which even now, were unbelievable.

All that surrounded me felt like it could disappear at any moment. My life felt surreal, as if I were an observer looking in on somebody else's life, one that certainly wasn't my own. There was no fear now; even the spiky sensations of panic had subsided and in their place came a practical need to find out what was going on and why. I had no control over what was happening; that much was clear.

I admitted to myself, as painful as it was, that I wasn't entirely without a degree of responsibility for what had happened – I had allowed myself to become vulnerable, completely reliant on others. I had no idea of how to run a home, no inkling as to who provided the services to the house, or even if there was a mortgage – if there was, I knew nothing of how much was due and when it was paid. I had let Mike deal with everything, and as a consequence, had become ignorant of my own life; it was an embarrassing and shameful moment of realisation.

I didn't even possess a bank account in my own name; credit cards, cash cards, everything had been linked to Mike's account on which I was just a card holder. He'd controlled all monetary needs, convincing me that there was no need for me to concern myself with the finances. Having never carried much cash, only cards, it was all too apparent in hindsight how controlled I was.

Getting back to the practicality of trying to contact my husband, I considered that no worthwhile contact could be made with America until after three or four o'clock in the afternoon. With it being lunchtime, I had to fill the time somehow. Collecting the dirty cups from the lounge, I made my way back to the kitchen. After rinsing the cups out, I sat at the breakfast bar staring once more at the empty space that was my home.

I realised that, before today, an outsider would probably have looked upon my life as resembling a fairytale, the perfect life. We loved and cherished our children desperately and, if I were honest, there had been very little confrontation the whole time Mike and I were married. In retrospect, I was now acutely aware that although the fifteen years had passed unremarkably, with no great incident and with speed, I knew very little of the Mike of today compared with the Mike of the past.

Sitting in the silence of the kitchen, I allowed myself to be transported back in time. In the very early days, I would spend hours getting ready to meet him. We had attended the same college, although we had taken different courses, and every meeting had been more exciting than the last.

It hadn't been long before we moved in together. Our first home was a small flea-bitten pit of a bedsit, but we loved it anyway – it was ours and we were happy. We would spend whole days making love, only broken by the occasional need to eat and drink. Hours would be spent talking about every subject imaginable. Mike had big plans to become rich and make it for himself. He was so driven and wanted to be the best at what he did, likely due to his parents. They were divorced, lived miles apart, and neither ever had any time for him; he was an after-thought at best. Subsequently, he learnt at an early age how to survive on his own and thrive. Eventually, they ceased all contact with him and he with them; I had never met them.

My own parents were middle-aged when they had me and both had passed away when I was still young. They had left sufficient funds for me to attend a good boarding school, along with a trust fund from their moderate savings to help me live independently when the need arose. There was no other family I could remember to speak of.

Though the memories of my parents were vague, I did recall a faded vision of my mother spending time with me, baking biscuits in the kitchen and playing card games on a large ornate rug in the living room. My memories of my father were even less clear; a tall, thick-set man wearing a mustard coloured cardigan, reading the paper in a red leather, wing-backed armchair and smoking a pipe.

I didn't recall any great illness or traumatic event to cause their demise, but remembered they died within a relatively short time of each other. From then, my life at Perse House Boarding School for Girls in nearby Cambridge, became my family and my home.

I met Marcia, or Marci as I often called her, as soon as I started at the school, being sat together for our first prep period. I was instantly in awe of her. Her superior air meant few of the girls even spoke to her, but I saw a different side to her; any derogatory remarks thrown her way were cut down with an excellent snide remark without a pause for breath.

On our first day, she smiled at me as I took my place at the desk next to hers. She then proceeded to extract, from her beautiful tote bag – which really should have been the standard issue satchel – two identical leather bound notebooks and passed one to me. This was the first of numerous gifts she would eventually bestow, but this was the most precious in my mind, and one that was both coveted and used every day.

Marci's world was like another universe to me. Everything had always been done for her, when she was at home anyway. Her meals were brought to her in her room, or dinner was announced by a bell if the family was having guests. She had more possessions than I could ever dream of; vast amounts of beautiful clothes and shoes that had never been worn occupied wardrobes the size of most people's living rooms.

Initially, Marci would seem cool towards people – it took some time, but I came to realise this was a survival strategy disguising nervousness, particularly if she was in a situation that was alien to her. She created a barrier that few people penetrated, but we became best friends. I never wanted anything from Marcia other than her friendship; maybe this was what she saw in me, and not in others. Marcia's parents were a high-flying couple, far too busy to spend much time with their daughter, so they welcomed me with open arms as the perfect companion for their daughter.

As we grew older, we spent weekends, holidays, and even Christmases together. The time to consider our paths upon leaving Perse House came, and I made the decision to go to a mainstream college. I studied Drama, finding it easy to pretend to be somebody else, having effectively honed the skills in Marcia's company and that of her parents. I was able to blend effortlessly with the set Marcia and her family kept and the escapism that drama afforded me was one of my greatest loves.

Marcia, much to the annoyance of her parents, decided to join the same college. She lost interest in most things very quickly though, so she studied a little of pretty much every course the establishment had to offer. Financing these educational forays was never an issue; Marcia's parents were insistent they pay my course fees and expenses as well, even though I was perfectly capable of it myself. I often thought they were grateful Marcia was occupied and therefore, out of their way.

The only occasion when parental objection became serious however, was when Marcia met Alex. Alex wasn't what they had in mind at all for their daughter; he was an ordinary boy who studied hard and had worked for everything he had. Their wish was for her to meet somebody titled, somebody with status – they realised all too late that attending college wasn't going to improve her chances of fulfilling their aspirations. Mike, Alex, Marcia and I made an inseparable, if somewhat odd, foursome.

Alex, unfortunately, loved Marcia far more than she him. She only had to click her fingers and Alex came running, and as such, Marcia continued her lifestyle of not having to lift a finger with Alex at her constant beck and call. When Alex announced he and Marcia were going to be married, Marcia's parents were furious. They believed Marcia was just being a little rebellious and would call an end to the charade eventually. Marcia, fed up with their attitude, was unrelenting – and in the ultimate act of defiance, the wedding went ahead. Alex had to work twice as hard to keep up with her materialistic demands and got very little in return.

Mike and Alex had studied the same engineering course together and had both gone on to become specialists in their fields. Alex had a flair for finances, honed partially from Marcia's excessive demands, whereas Mike was particularly cunning when it came to negotiation – together, their first large, lucrative contract was won.

Their company, Claremont and Weston, was born and they were in business. As the business grew, more staff, larger offices and many more clients were all attained, and as such, longer hours had to be put in; that was the beginning of Mike and I drifting apart.

***

Sitting at the barren breakfast bar, thinking about the past, I had to acknowledge I had made no effort to stop the rift forming; in fact, I had allowed it to happen so I could accommodate my own frivolous indulgences. I was to almost as much to blame as Mike was.

Looking up at the kitchen clock, which was in the shape of a cat, black, with its bright green eyes moving from left to right in time with the seconds passing, I was surprised to see it was almost time for me to collect Alice and Phoebe from school. I had been thinking for hours and my head ached. I saw through the large kitchen window overlooking the courtyard that my car had been returned, having been unaware of its arrival while I'd been lost in thought.

Picking up my bag and Mike's mobile phone, I went out into the rapidly cooling afternoon. My mind was racing. What do I tell the girls? Should I tell them anything? If I pretended nothing had happened, how long could I keep it up for? Dozens of questions, all with no answers. I wondered if it might be easier for me to say Mike was away on business. He always brought gifts home for the girls and they, in turn, forgave him his absence. My decision was made. I would act as normal as possible, making up excuses until I had spoken with Mike directly.

Even now, I swung from wanting to forgive him and return to our status quo, to wanting to almost kill him. I was awash with conflicting emotions, never considering the decision may have already been made for me.

I recalled the look on Marcia's face when I told her about the unpaid bills and about the alleged sale of the house. She'd been embarrassed, but she'd also had the look of pity – she might well have looked more comfortable if I had admitted I'd found Mike in bed with another woman. I wondered if Marcia was better equipped to deal with infidelity than she was to deal with financial digressions; so long as there was money in the bank, Marcia was happy. A life without money was one I couldn't ever imagine Marcia being able to comprehend or contemplate.

Sadly, it dawned on me that if I were about to experience some financial challenges or difficulties, Marcia would likely make herself scarce. With this thought, I felt alone.

5.

As I pulled onto the school's driveway, I was somewhat alarmed at the lack of recollection of any aspect of the journey I had just made. I decided to park under a large oak tree at the farthest corner of the car park. Although I had joined the collection of Bentleys, Jaguars, BMWs, the odd Maybach and various four-wheel drive vehicles waiting to be loaded up with children, I wasn't in the mood to engage in idle conversation.

I used my interior rear-view mirror to watch the proceedings without having to stand amongst it. Nannies stood around in their wellington boots and Barbour jackets waiting for their charges to emerge. They tended to stand in little groups, discussing their employer's latest acquisitions, be it equine, property or vehicular – or just gossip to help time pass.

It never ceased to amaze me how nannies were almost always awarded a four-wheel drive vehicle as part of their employment package – as if they had a great off road journey to and from school. In reality, almost all of them came from smart, gated developments where a spot of mud on the drive was a cause for concern and always dealt with immediately. The only journeys they undertook were to the school or nursery and back.

Possibly the odd riding lesson or after-school activity, maybe a shopping trip or two – regardless, it certainly wasn't a journey that was likely to include traversing a one in four gradient on the way to Waitrose.

Slowly, children began to emerge from the collection of impressive Victorian buildings that made up the school. The younger pupils, dragging their standard issue satchels along the ground, resplendent in their sporting of half-on, half-off blazers while the older students walked very slowly and chatted animatedly to each other on their way toward the waiting vehicles. I was awestruck as to how the teenage contingency of the school looked far older than their years. Particularly the girls, who could have quite easily have passed for early twenties with very little effort.

Cars began to pull away, until there were only a few left, giving an abandoned feel to the car park. A growing sense of foreboding began spreading through my body, my mouth was dry and woollen; the girls should have been out by now. I racked my brain, trying to remember if there had been any netball, hockey or gymnastic practices I had forgotten about – it wouldn't have been the first time. I waited five more minutes, frantically flicking through my hastily retrieved diary, looking for clues. Unable to stand the tension any longer, I almost ran to the main school building.

As I entered, I caught a glimpse of Mrs Anderson, the headmistress, going into her office. Apart from her, the area was deserted. Quickly knocking on the headmistress's office door, I heard the footsteps of the occupant walking towards me from the other side. Before the door opened fully, I heard someone screaming the words, "Where are Phoebe and Alice Weston?" It took a moment to recognise my own voice, my emotions having gotten the better of me.

"Mrs Weston, I would appreciate it if you didn't yell at me as soon as I open my door." Her calm voice demanded respect.

"I don't care what you would and would not appreciate. Where are my daughters?"

"Your husband collected them earlier today, to take them on holiday. Is there a problem?" Still, the headmistress was unflustered.

"Well, of course there's a problem – what holiday? And why did you let him take them?" Spitting out the words, I was already blaming her wholly for everything. The tears burned behind my already stinging eyes.

"Your husband requested some time ago to take the children out of school for a two-week holiday. I granted the request as there are no exams for a while and their study, as you know, is well above average." Again, her tone remained even, displaying no emotion.

"There's no holiday, my children are missing, along with my husband. We must call the police." My voice was faltering and the rage that had been coursing through my charged body began to ebb away slowly, leaving me trembling. Looking into the older woman's eyes, I pleaded with my own, unable to speak further.

Mrs Anderson, a sturdy woman of some fifty-plus years, must have been moved by my dreadful appearance; it was obvious something had happened.

"Mrs Weston, would you like to see the letter requesting permission for your children to be excused?" she offered, studying my distraught face.

"Yes, I bloody well would!" My temper spiked again uncontrollably, causing me to question my own sanity in the moment following.

I followed Mrs Anderson further into her office. She continued through an adjoining door, gone for a moment, before returning with a piece of paper that was instantly recognisable to me as the headed paper of Claremont and Weston. She handed the paper to me and my blood ran cold; the date on the letter was over five weeks previous. I felt like a knife had been thrust into my heart and, for a moment, I was unable to breathe. It was a simply worded request, asking that the girls be excused from school attendance in order to go on a family holiday. I read and re-read the single paragraph.

Five weeks ago, my husband had planned to take my children away from me. Although having accepted life wasn't at its best between Mike and I, I could never have imagined he considered it so bad that he would want to hurt me so much. Gradually, I became aware of a vague murmur in the background – it was Mrs Anderson talking to me.

"Mrs Weston, whatever your family circumstances, they are entirely your own affair. My concern is for your children. As you can imagine, we have numerous pupils whose parents are divorced or separated. As long as the children are happy, and well cared for, we do not involve ourselves in their home life." She paused for a moment, before continuing, "We have found that it's not unusual to receive a request from a sole parent to take their children on holiday. An awful lot of parents are unable to take the time off together these days." Then, "It's obvious to me that your children adore their father and there wasn't anything in the least bit sinister about today."

"Mrs Anderson, you have no idea how wrong that statement is." I knew I sounded desperate. The headmistress regarded me with a quizzical look.

"What exactly has happened today, Mrs Weston?"

"In simple terms, my husband has disappeared, along with my children. The likelihood is that I'm losing, if not lost already, my home, and I can't seem to do a thing about it." Unable to stop myself, I sarcastically added, "Apart from that, everything is fine – nothing sinister here." I wanted to rage, to blame the world and everyone in it for what was happening to me. My head swam for a moment and a strange, surreal sensation came over me. The floor came up to meet me; then, darkness.

"Mrs Weston. Mrs Weston, can you hear me?"

"Yes, yes, I'm sorry – I must have – have – Oh, I don't feel very well." There were white, flashing flecks before my eyes. I could hear my own voice, but it sounded distant, not in sync with my mouth.

"Take your time and I'll get you some sweet tea," the kind voice said.

I was helped to a sitting position with my back against a filing cabinet, and I tried to focus. The headmistress patted my shoulder gently and then disappeared again. The white flecks were slowing, and the fog in my head was gradually lifting.

At last, I was able to focus on the large china teacup being offered to me and I carefully took a sip. The tea was strong, and very sweet. As awful as it was, it was soothing, nonetheless. Mrs Anderson sat opposite me on a chair she had drawn up, allowing me to collect myself before speaking.

"Mrs Weston, if you tell me exactly what has happened, I might be able to help."

I thought for a moment. I hadn't anything to lose telling this kind woman, almost a stranger really, all that had happened. Although I was uncomfortable admitting it to myself, she may be able to help; she was the only person that had offered. After a few more sips of tea, I felt I was able to tell her the whole story without losing too much control. Once started, I felt an overwhelming sense of relief at telling somebody everything – every thought, every emotion. When I finally finished, I was drained, but also felt the process had been cathartic somehow.

The silence was deafening. Eventually Mrs Anderson spoke. "I think your suspicions are founded and I can understand your feelings when you arrived at the school this afternoon. However, the school cannot stop either parent seeing their children, unless it has very good cause, predominantly a legal cause. The children are not officially missing; I have notification of their removal from school for a holiday," she finished apologetically.

I knew she was telling the truth - the police would be powerless, not being able to get involved unless there was reason to believe the disappearance was a kidnapping. Furthermore, to all but me, everything was in order.

"I also don't feel your children are in any danger with your husband, nor, I suspect, do you," she added softly. "However, I do believe you must try and contact your husband as soon as possible to try and make sense of what has happened and, of course, confirm the children's wellbeing. Do you have that New York phone number with you?"

"Yes, yes I do." My mouth was dry again and my words barely audible. The stabbing pain in my heart, the pain of loss, was overwhelming. I wasn't sure I could move, or even that I wanted to.

My feelings must have been obvious for the headmistress to see; she addressed me like she would a pupil needing coaching to reach a potential she knew they had, even if they didn't.

"Why not try and call from my phone here? I'll go into the office next door and give you some privacy. Give it a try now, while you're here."

"Thank you so much." Again, the words were barely audible, my throat constricted trying to control the emotion threatening to overwhelm me again.

As the headmistress left the office, she turned and smiled gently at me.

"I'm only next door if you need me."

Then she was gone. There were now new questions – how had Mike gotten our daughters to go with him without questioning my whereabouts? How long had Mike been planning this, and why? I felt beaten and alone. Wearily, I picked up the phone from its cradle on the large desk, drawing it closer to me as I sat in the large leather chair and dialled the New York number. It was answered almost instantly, and I tried to sound as casual and confident as possible.

"Good morning, my name is Mrs Weston. My husband is due to see Mr Simco, in the next day or two, and I wondered if I could leave a message for him when he arrives?"

I could hear the polite receptionist tapping away at, what I assumed, was a computer.

"Ah yes, Mrs Weston, I see the appointment here, it's for tomorrow at two. Oh, just one moment –

there's a further note to say your husband cancelled the appointment. He's due to call us back to re-schedule."

My heart plummeted, and I fought a wave of nausea.

"Did he give any reason at all?" I continued, not really caring now how odd the question sounded – I needed to know.

"No, ma'am, I'm afraid I don't have any further comments written down here and, unfortunately, I wasn't the person who took the call. Is everything okay, ma'am?"

"Yes, yes. I'm sorry to have wasted your time."

"Not at all, ma'am, have a nice day."

Slowly, I replaced the receiver and allowed myself to give in to the sobs I'd held at bay. Beginning to retch, I felt as though my heart might explode out of my chest; I was now questioning if the relief of death would have been welcome. I don't know how long I was slumped over the desk, giving in to how wretched I felt, only being drawn back to the present by the return of Mrs Anderson.

"I take it wasn't good news?" she questioned delicately.

"He had an appointment but cancelled it. He hasn't rescheduled a new one. Any trail I had appears to have gone dead." A whisper was all I could muster.

"Can I drive you home? You can collect your car tomorrow if you like."

"Thank you, that's very kind of you. I don't think I should drive right now."

I didn't feel capable of anything. My world had come to a grinding halt. The need to hold my children, all consuming. I felt huge pressure on my chest, making me struggle for breath; the sense of loss suffocated me.

The drive back to the house was a quiet one, I spoke only to give directions. By the time we reached home I was exhausted. Mrs Anderson took the key from me, my hands shaking too much to get it into the lock, and let us in. The need to be alone was overpowering, but out of politeness I offered to make tea. Thankfully, the headmistress must have sensed my mood and graciously declined, explaining there were teacher's assessments to write, amongst other tasks that required her immediate attention. We made arrangements to collect my car the following morning.

I closed the door, after watching her drive off and disappear into the distance. The time was five thirty. My children, had they been home, would have been about to start dinner, or at least a snack. The television would have been blaring, along with the audio system, and there would have been a pile of books, bags and coats at the bottom of the stairs. General shouting and laughing, punctuated by the odd bout of bickering would have continued throughout the house until bedtime.

Instead, just deafening silence. My knees gave way and with my back to the back of the front door, I sank to the floor. I allowed the tears to flow freely and my sorrow came over me in great crashing waves. My heart was broken; I was grief stricken and alone.

Consciousness left me, but I don't recall when, only returning with the slow realisation there was an almighty banging sound coming from somewhere. It was so loud, I could almost feel the vibration in my head, an onslaught to my senses. The cold marble floor had turned my cheek numb where I had eventually lain. There was a dull ache in my legs, and the stinging in my eyes was worse than ever from the constant crying. Slowly, I gathered myself together, the banging getting louder. Eventually it registered there was someone thumping on the front door.

My initial, albeit fleeting, thought, was that it was Mike and the children returning home. The misery that accompanied the almost simultaneous realisation that this was unlikely enveloped me once more.

"Who is it?" I was irritated by the intrusion, wanting to be alone in my grief.

"It's Alex, can I come in?"

"What do you want?" I asked. I didn't want to see or speak to anybody.

"I need to talk to you."

I was a little surprised by the insistence in his voice and sensed from his tone he wasn't likely to go away. Pulling myself groggily to my feet, I opened the door.

Alex stood in the doorway, looking like he had slept in his suit after having received a large electric shock. His hair stood almost on end, I guessed as a result of continuously running fingers through it, as was his habit when under pressure or in deep concentration. His tie was loosely knotted and hung haphazardly around his neck, resembling a hangman's noose. The whole ensemble gave the impression he was living on the street.

"What time is it?" I mumbled, feeling I probably looked no better myself.

"Two in the morning," came the response.

"What can be so bloody important that you need to talk to me at two in the morning?" No sooner had the words left my lips than I knew he must have news. My heart leapt and my breath caught in my throat. "Have you heard from Mike? Are the girls okay? Where are they? What did they say?" I knew I sounded half-crazed, firing questions and not waiting for answers.

"I'm sorry, it's not news from Mike or the girls."

"What then?" I demanded. Nothing else mattered.

"You might want to sit down, Julia." A chill ran up my spine as we moved to the lounge.

"I had some visitors at the office today. They were from Inland Revenue and the Fraud Squad."

"So, what has this got to do with me?" I was impatient now – if Alex had come to talk about anything other than my family, why should I care?

Looking gaunt, Alex continued. "It would appear Claremont and Weston have been under investigation for some time. They've been monitoring our dealings, and our accounting records have been scrutinised for the last two years. Money's gone missing." The grey pallor Alex had arrived with worsened. I was astounded.

"I thought you took care of the financial side of the business," I stated, in an accusing tone.

"I did, until about three years ago, when Mike suggested we use a firm of accountants he knew. This would mean more of my time was freed up for other aspects of the business – at the rate we were growing, it seemed like an excellent idea."

"So, what happened to this money?"

Alex relayed everything he had been told that afternoon: Mike had been winning contracts and requesting advances in order to cover materials, development work and research for them. This money had been paid into an account, which the authorities were still trying to trace. The figures that were declared on the company tax returns were, consequently, incorrect. The upshot was that the company – therefore, Alex and Mike – owed Inland Revenue huge amounts of money in unpaid tax. The money, it would appear, had disappeared along with Mike.

I couldn't believe my ears; why would Mike do this? He was always on the straight-and-narrow, the one who did everything by the book. I recalled the phone conversation with the mobile phone people and the unpaid invoices; nothing made any sense. Who was this man? Not the man I would have laid my life down for, the man who would have done the same for me – that man had disappeared.

"Mike's been embezzling money from his – our – own company. I can't understand why he'd do this," continued Alex frustratedly, looking bewildered. He went on to tell me how Inland Revenue had seized the company in its entirety; all assets had been taken, all bank accounts, frozen, including personal ones, and all customer contracts had been cancelled. He went on to explain that, because insurances wouldn't be paid due to the investigation, the company would now be sued by its customers for breach of contract. The offices had been closed and the staff had been released, unpaid. Alex began to ramble and mumble incoherently.

I had to know. With a false calm, I asked, "How much are they talking about, Alex?"

"Four point seven million pounds." The words were barely a whisper

I froze.

"What?" My voice had the high pitch tone of shock. I stood numbly for a moment, before molten anger took over my body, taking me by surprise. How *dare* Mike do this to me – to us all?

"If Inland Revenue has worked out they're owed four, no, almost five million pounds, I haven't even attempted to work out how much Mike actually took."

Alex was now running his fingers through his hair repeatedly, the quick, desperate tugging motions making it even more dishevelled.

"Have you told Marcia about this?"

I truly felt sorry for Alex now, guessing the response wouldn't have been supportive, nor comforting, for Alex.

"I have. She's left me. Told me in no uncertain terms that she wouldn't live amongst this sort of 'scandal'. Caught the next flight out to Monte Carlo to join her parents on the yacht." His short, impassive tone made me wince.

"Christ, Alex, I'm so sorry. I knew absolutely nothing about this I swear." For some inexplicable reason, I felt responsible for the position Mike had placed us in. I noticed a distant look in Alex's eyes; something had shattered within him.

"I knew you wouldn't, I just had to tell you and, in a selfish way, ask that if you do speak to Mike, please let me know. The other reason was to warn you; you may have a visit from the people who were at the office today."

I think we both knew I would probably be the last person Mike would be contacting, though neither of us said so. When I mentioned the New York phone conversation and the cancelled appointment, Alex's face fell further. It was obvious Mike was in no hurry to return home. A silence fell between us, both absorbing the new information.

Looking at Alex slumped in the sofa across from me, he looked like he had aged ten years in a day. It couldn't have been easy for him to come to terms with the revelation that his business partner and best friend had robbed him of his livelihood, his wife and his life, in one swift moment.

Alex had no children of his own to consider, just his wife and his business. Both had been snatched away from him as quickly as all that was precious to me had disappeared. We had nothing more to say to each other, both lost in our own misery.

I had no recollection of what time we eventually fell asleep; we had made our way to the kitchen for coffee and had fallen asleep, heads lowered onto the breakfast bar. Upon waking and feeling worse than ever, both physically and mentally, I excused myself and went to take a shower.

Studying my face in the mirror, my mood matched my reflection: dull and defeated. Entering the shower, it felt good to have the hot water pounding against my skin, washing away the grime of the last twenty-four hours. For what felt like an eternity, I stood beneath the torrent of water, not wanting to move, trying desperately to push the sorrow to the back of my confused mind. Eventually, I left the safe haven of the cubicle, dried myself and dressed quickly.

Returning to the kitchen, I saw Alex was up and making coffee. His pallor was worse than the previous day, his eyes dark, dead, and his actions robotic. I wasn't comfortable broaching the subject, but knew I had no choice.

"Did Mike mention a holiday at all to you, Alex?"

There was no answer and I wasn't even sure Alex had heard me. I knew I had to start looking for Mike myself and couldn't waste any more time.

"Can I have the keys to the office, Alex?"

"It's no good, there's nothing there. They've probably changed the locks by now." Alex's emotionless tone made the hairs stand on the back of my neck, though I wasn't sure why.

"I don't mind taking a chance – I just want to snoop around anyway. I promise I won't tell anyone you gave me the keys if I'm stopped or asked."

"Whatever." Alex threw me the keys. I had a bad feeling about the state of Alex's mind, but I had to do all I could to find my children and there was no time to waste.

6.

Driving to the Claremont and Weston offices, I made a mental note of things to look out for. Recent correspondence relating to travel, travel agent brochures – pretty much anything that might indicate a holiday was top of my list.

The traffic was unusually heavy for the time of day and the journey was taking longer than I expected. I was feeling the probing twinges of tension beginning to spread across my shoulders and towards my neck, making my jaw set and teeth clench together. The bad driving of other motorists was beginning to give me a headache. I knew I needed to be as clear-headed as possible and desperately tried to keep calm and focused.

As I pulled into the car park, my heart sank. What was once a busy area, with an incessant multitude of people milling around, was now completely deserted. I recalled that on the odd occasion when I came to the office before, there would be office workers enjoying a cigarette break, people crossing the road to get a sandwich from the nearby delicatessen, or collecting their dry cleaning from the next building – there had always been a steady ebb and flow of people arriving and leaving.

The sight before me now was of desolation; all that was left was an overflowing bin near the entrance and snack wrappers being blown across the empty car park. The slightest sound seemed to echo, exaggerated in its loudness, the acoustics heightened by the open space and tall buildings. Quickly, I locked the car and made my way to the rear entrance of the company's impressive building. The lock turned easily with the first key I chose from Alex's bunch. I offered up a prayer of thanks – the investigators must have already taken what they needed, the locks not having yet been changed.

As quickly and light-footed as possible, I took the stairs two at a time towards the executive level, consciously choosing to not use the elevators, feeling they may draw attention to my presence – I also didn't want to get stuck if there was a problem. This was where Alex, Mike and their assistants had their offices. It had been a while since I had been to the building and I wasn't sure which office belonged to Mike; they all looked the same without their occupants. After going into each, I was still none the wiser. Retracing my steps, I recognized an umbrella hanging from a large ornate coat stand. It was a Christmas present from Phoebe and Alice to Mike a couple of years previous, being conspicuous only for the fact the handle was a large wooden duck head painted bright yellow.

Holding my breath, I tried the handle of the door to the inner office. It wasn't locked and opened easily. I slowly exhaled, letting myself in and closing the door as silently as possible behind me. I was still creeping about, though I was, by now, quite sure nobody was about.

At first glance, the desk and cabinets looked completely clear. There were no personal items or memorabilia to signify to whom the office had once belonged, save for the umbrella. Inexplicably, I felt treacherous as I systematically began opening drawers and cupboards. There were large cherry wood cabinets on two walls, a very large window on the third wall and a further office to the other side.

I sat in Mike's high-backed leather chair behind his desk and pushed gently with my feet; this afforded me a panoramic view of his office. As I began my second full rotation, beginning to feel a little dizzy, something caught my eye. There was a corner of something hanging over the lip of one of the taller cabinets, by just a fraction, only being noticeable as there was nothing else to be seen. I had to stand on my tiptoes to reach the edge, and with some effort, could just about grasp the corner of the object between my fingertips.

I could feel the paper was glossy and I hung on to it until I could gain more leverage, grasping enough of the paper to drag what, I could now see, looked very much like a magazine cover towards me. By pulling hard on what I could of the magazine corner, it came crashing to the floor, with what sounded like a small explosion in the silence of the building.

For some reason, I stood motionless, as if expecting someone to come rushing in to see what all the noise was about. After reprimanding myself in whispered tones, I sat back down in the chair. Slowly turning the cover of the magazine, I couldn't believe my luck; it was a holiday brochure. Unfortunately, the elation was short lived. The brochure was for America, but the choice of destinations vast. If Mike had taken the girls to America, they could be anywhere. In a country so large, I questioned whether I would have any hope of ever finding them.

Turning the pages, I read about two adventure package holidays, fourteen days in New England, fourteen days at Disney World, fourteen nights in Las Vegas – the list went on and on. The more I read, the more hopeless things looked. I had looked through pretty much all of the brochure and was beginning to slip back into despondency when I came across some figures on the back cover written in blue ballpoint pen. The figures were *2400, 600* and *600*, arranged in a sum with the largest figure at the top of the calculation. Somebody had been calculating figures, but why? I was beginning to feel I was maybe reading too much into something so small, in my desperation to find answers and my children.

An idea came suddenly; maybe the figures represented were an adult fare and two children's fares for one of the packages in the brochure. Pushing my incredulity at possibly creating something from nothing out of my mind, I decided to take the brochure home to study in more detail.

Relief flooded through me upon leaving the building and getting back into the comfort and safety of my car. It was unnerving being in a building that was completely empty, yet had evidence of recent life within its walls; half-empty coffee cups dotted about and post-it notes stuck to desks with messages for people to call. It was as if all the people had been erased, but the background of the picture remained untouched. It reminded me of a stage set in a theatre, when the play has long finished, and the audience gone home.

The drive back home passed without any awareness. My mind was racing. When had Mike taken his passport? That was a silly question, Mike always travelled and probably kept it with him at all times. What about the girls' passports? They had been issued some time ago, were they even still in date? Had he renewed them, and if so, when? The one answer I couldn't envision however, was how on earth Mike had managed to get our children to go away with him without them once mentioning anything to me – had it been a last-minute act, or had they known for some time? What could he possibly have said to them?

The thing was, they could just as easily be holidaying somewhere in England, or any other country for that matter. It was only the brochure that had offered up the possibility of a holiday in America, which didn't give much to go on. The more I dwelled on the information I had gathered, the worse I felt.

7.

As I pulled into the courtyard at the front of the house, I noticed Alex's car had now gone from the driveway. I let myself into the house and went directly to the kitchen. It was the only room I now felt comfortable in, because all the other rooms held memories of being occupied by my family, and I felt the pain too great whenever I passed through them. I had to admit, until now, the kitchen was almost unknown to me. I made a sandwich for lunch, reminding myself that I had to eat to stay strong – being strong was paramount in getting my children back. I forced myself to eat the whole thing, though it tasted of sawdust.

Alex had obviously decided to go home. The note he left said he would call by soon. The post remained where I had left it, in a neat pile, unopened. Deciding to go through it, I was able to discard the majority as being junk mail, but there was one letter in a heavyweight cream coloured envelope that I didn't recognise, addressed to Mr & Mrs Weston. I opened it.

As I read the contents, my heart began to race, and the familiar sense of panic began to choke me once more. It was official – the house had been sold. The letter was from our solicitors confirming the sale price and stating a completion and moving in date for the new owners. I had four days to get out of the house.

Unable to move, shock rocked me to my core and rendered me incapable of thinking clearly. My mind began racing, trying to recall signing anything at all that may have related to the house. It was true, Mike did sometimes thrust forms under my nose and ask me to 'autograph here', but I never read anything I signed – what reason did I have to? I acknowledged, ashamedly, that I should have – God only knew what else I'd unwittingly put my name to. Four days to find somewhere else to live, with no money and no idea where to start. The only friend I considered myself to have previously was now safely ensconced in the Mediterranean.

I knew the only way to survive now was to deal with one issue at a time. My only priority was to find my children; everything else would have to wait. I took the brochure I had found in Mike's office and began to re-examine it. I was only able to match up the figures written on the back of the brochure to two packages, which I allowed myself to think was at least a start.

One package was for fourteen nights in Las Vegas; the other was a fourteen-day fly-drive to Orlando. A Disney Park pass was included for any children travelling. Considering Phoebe and Alice's ages and the gambling laws in America, amongst other things, I hedged my bets on the Disney trip.

At least twice I told myself I was reading more into a single scribbled sum than was sensible, but what more had I to lose? All I had to do now was to ring the travel agent's number, helpfully provided by the large sticker slapped on the front of the brochure. The drawback was I had no way to make the call, before remembering Mike's mobile phone – it may have been disconnected along with everything else by now, but it was worth a try.

I retrieved the mobile from one of the work surfaces and dialled. So far, so good. As the phone was ringing at the other end, I began running through the story I would give to whoever answered; it had to sound reasonably plausible. My heart was beating so loud, I thought it was in danger of giving me away to whoever answered the phone.

"Good afternoon, Robin's Travel Agents, how may I help you?"

I jumped at the initial introduction, but by the time the lady had finished, I had calmed myself a little.

"Good afternoon. Yes, I wonder if you could help me?"

"I'll try, madam." The voice already sounded bored, which to my mind was a bonus – bored employees often didn't care enough to withhold information. That was my theory anyway.

"I would like to find out some travel details for my husband and two children."

"Madam, are you a member of the travelling party?"

I thought I might laugh. "No, I'm not, in fact, I'm not even sure my family are travelling at all but would like to check if I may." I realised how lame the conversation sounded and felt the travel agent was losing patience.

"I'm sorry, but if you're not a member of the travelling party, I'm not allowed to give you any information."

There went my theory. My frustration with the situation made me lose my patience.

"If I were a member of the travelling party, the likelihood would be that I already have the information I need and wouldn't need to call you. Don't you think?"

"I'm sorry, madam, that's our policy."

Wanting to slap the smugness out of the agent's voice, thinking violence would have allowed me to vent at least, I instead hung up, no longer having the energy to argue. Tears choked me; all I wanted, all I needed to know, was where my children and husband were. The tears eventually gave way to sleep, in the slumped position over the counter which I seemed to have adopted lately.

When I woke, it was dark outside and almost as dark inside the house until I turned on the lights in the kitchen. Looking at my watch, I saw I had slept for some time. I knew now that I would have to be devious in order to get the information I needed. *To catch a snake, you had to be a snake*, I told myself. The travel agent was an important key; I would have to call them again. I recalled the girl's voice and thought I'd recognise it if she were to answer the phone a second time – I would hang up and try again if this happened.

This time, the call had to be planned, better thought through. My story would be I had been added as an extra person to the travelling party at the last moment. I knew this happened sometimes, having travelled with Mike on some of his work trips in the early days. The extra person is treated as an entirely separate booking, with a different booking reference, invoice and ticket. If the enquiry was kept simple and I acted a little dumb, there was a possibility the agent may bring up the first booking.

If not, I would be back to square one, but I pushed that thought to the back of my mind. Positivity was what was needed to make things happen; there were enough odds stacked against me by others, I didn't need my own doubts adding to them. Looking at the clock, I knew I only had forty-five minutes left of the working day. I made coffee, unable to bring myself to eat but thinking the caffeine would keep me going, I braced myself, took a deep breath and dialled the number for the second time.

It was a good start – a male voice answered this time and I let him finish his introduction. Feeling surprisingly assertive and confident, I began.

"Good afternoon. I'm led to believe that there's a booking for me to join my family in America, but to be honest, I'm not sure of the departure time. I think it's ticket on departure." I hoped I sounded clipped and to the point.

"What is the name, please?"

"Weston, Mr and Mrs Weston," I added the Mister in the hope that a booking would be found in Mike's name.

"Could you confirm your address please?" I gave our address and waited, my heart pounding in my ears. I held my breath and prayed silently.

"And the departure date please?"

Bile rose in my mouth. I hadn't expected to get this far and hadn't really thought too much about the departure date. Trying to remember what Mrs Anderson had told me, I decided all I could do was guess.

"Umm, I think it's the 11th." I tried to sound deliberately vague, as if dates always evaded me.

"Ah yes, I see the booking now. Your husband and two other passengers flew out yesterday evening."

I held back the sob which was threatening to escape. "Yes, that's right," was all I could mumble.

"But I'm afraid I don't seem to have any booking for you, Mrs Weston." The tone was puzzled and slightly apologetic, as if the fault was his. I could hear him tapping away furiously, giving me a moment to gather my composure.

"My husband promised to make the arrangements for me as I was out of town, I'll have to sort them out myself." I aimed to sound agitated, as if this was a simple, yet annoying, inconvenience. I was beginning to panic again when the operator spoke.

"I can check availability for Orlando International Airport for you now, if you don't mind holding for a moment or two?" I could have kissed him, barely containing an excited screech. This stranger had unwittingly given me the missing clue. Now, I was smiling into the handset.

"Thanks, that would be great." I prayed the battery on Mike's phone lasted. Again, the tapping of keys commenced with renewed vigour.

"I can get you on a flight tomorrow morning, if that is any help?"

"That would be terrific, thanks."

"Lovely, may I have a credit card number for payment?"

I flipped to the first credit card in my wallet which, for once, was nearby and read out a number. More furious tapping on the keyboard ensued.

"I'm sorry, there appears to be a problem with that card, is there another I can try for you?"

Even reading out the number on the second card, I knew it was useless. Remembering Alex's words, all the accounts had been frozen. There was no way of getting a plane ticket. I was dying inside; the grief was crippling and I felt a familiar vice-like sensation around my throat, choking me. The kind, if slightly embarrassed, tone of the operator came back on to tell me the card had been declined again. Pursuing the matter was pointless. I thanked the man for his help and hung up.

There were no more tears, just an overwhelming feeling of desolation and helplessness, my eyes burning from staring, unseeing, into the gloom. When my eyes could focus no more, I went wearily upstairs. Opening Alice and Phoebe's bedroom door and turning on the light, I stood, absorbing every detail. It was all so much more important now. I never understood why my daughters chose to share a room, but they had. Even now they were teenagers, they had stayed together. They had their fights and squabbles, but they always patched things up. They were there for each other and I was deeply grateful for it.

I knew Mike would never harm the girls. He loved them dearly, but what he had said to them, I couldn't imagine. Whatever it was, I would tell them the truth when the time came, when I had them in my arms again. At least they had each other.

Chilled to the bone, the house feeling so much colder minus my family, I went to my bedroom to get another sweater. As I was rummaging around in the wardrobes for an old favourite – a dark grey, oversized cashmere that had seen better days, long assigned to the back shelves – my arm knocked down an old shoe box.

It must have been stuffed behind the front row of folded knitwear.

Having finally found the much-loved sweater, which I instantly pulled on, wrapping the extra folds around myself, I picked up the shoe box and went into the children's room. I had no new ideas and needed to feel close to my children, if only by surrounding myself with their stuffed toys and curling up in their duvets. I didn't want to cry anymore; I wanted to be strong. Looking at the box closely, I saw it was beaten and well worn, the shoe shop it came from long since closed down. I didn't even remember the shoes it had once housed, yet I was intrigued as to what was in it now.

Taking the lid off, I emptied the box in the well my crossed legs created. Nothing really caught my eye; there were some old key rings with picture of Marcia and I pulling faces when we were schoolgirls, old cinema tickets, bus tickets, and small furry animals I had obviously been collecting at some point. In the bottom of the box, snugly wedged, were some old exercise books, English, History and some sketches I had drawn in a long-forgotten art class.

Right at the bottom of the pile was a small grey book, not particularly thick, but worn and dog-eared. At first, I wasn't sure what it was until I opened it. It was an old savings account book, still in my maiden name; more importantly, in very faded type, it showed a balance of two thousand, seven hundred and sixty-two pounds.

I was shocked to hear a loud laugh emerge, making me jump. I then realised the laugh was my own and, after a pause, I was laughing hysterically, allowing myself this one moment of joy and optimism. Eventually calming down, I studied the text again and regarded the date. It was, at the very least, sixteen years old. I was unable to recall the last time I had used the book. I felt a small ray of hope – maybe I now had finances, but to what extent?

There was always the possibility that I had used the money, and the book was incorrect – I racked my brain but couldn't remember a thing about it. Not long after being married, with Mike's business taking off, money became less and less of note. This was around the same time I allowed myself to become ignorant. Equally, I couldn't remember having made any specific purchases around that time which may have used up the money

Looking at the shocking pink neon clock on the bedroom wall, I saw it was now far too late to do anything about my discovery, but first thing in the morning, I would get myself to the building society and have the book updated. I also found an old library card and some other forms of identification; thankfully nothing contained any photos.

The account, being in my maiden name, I prayed would have remained untouched by the financial freeze issued by the tax officials. I promised myself I would see my children soon. This had become my mantra. The promise was to myself and my babies, wherever they were. It kept me focused.

Before retiring, I made a list of things to do the next day. Top of the list was to try and get a cheque for the flight to Orlando. Following that, I wanted to take out as much cash as the building society would allow. Perhaps, if I played it well, I could withdraw a thousand pounds; I'd just have to wait and see. I hoped and prayed there actually was money in the account – so much was riding on it that I couldn't allow myself to think otherwise. Lastly, I had to find somewhere to live, or at least store some furniture, as I didn't want to have to give up everything. A final thought passed through my mind before my body slipped into the realms of sleep; Alex hadn't called by. I rationalised that he had an awful lot on his mind – he was probably just busy trying to salvage what he could of his life. Nodding to myself, I drifted off to sleep, passbook held tightly in my hand.

I was woken by an incessant hammering on the door. I was cautious of any contact with the outside world right now, not quite sure what would – or could – happen next. I listened, and waited, hoping whoever it was would go away. I wondered for a second if it was Alex returning, but for some reason I didn't think so. The hammering continued. Begrudgingly, I made my way to the front bedroom to see if I could covertly see who it was before considering answering the door.

I was startled to see two police cars. Dread flooded my body. I ran downstairs and threw open the door, allowing the icy blast of air coupled with panic, to wake me fully. The two police officers were as startled by my actions as I was to see them.

"Mrs Weston?" the taller of the two questioned.

"Yes, is it about my children, my husband? Please God, tell me they're safe." I blurted the words hurriedly. The officers looked puzzled.

"Mrs Weston, do you know of a Mr Alex Claremont?"

My heart froze, my whole body suddenly incredibly heavy.

"Yes, yes I do. He's my husband's business partner and he's married to my best friend."

"I'm afraid we have some bad news. Could we come in for a moment?"

My shoulders ached with tension and I showed the officers to the lounge. They gestured for me to sit down; I gladly complied, every limb dense with stress and anxiety. Finally, the smaller, younger officer spoke.

"I'm sorry to inform you like this, but Mr Claremont was found dead earlier this morning in his car, close to the local woods." The policeman looked a little relieved, as if he had got the worst over with.

"But I saw him only—" I stopped, sobs wracking my body, unable to finish my sentence. I cried for some time, lost in a haze, grieving, not even noticing the officers in the room with me. Eventually, I calmed a little, the sobs subsiding.

"Mrs Weston, Mr Claremont left this for you." An envelope was handed to me, having been opened but re-sealed. "Mrs Weston, what can you tell us about Mr Claremont? Do you know anything about the state of his mind, was he worried about anything? He succumbed to carbon monoxide poisoning and it would appear he took his own life,' finished the officer. The officers sounded too clinical, too routine and I felt my anger rising.

"My husband is under investigation for tax evasion, fraud and embezzlement. Alex's life's work had been destroyed by somebody he trusted, someone he regarded as his best friend, as well as his business partner. His wife deserted him as soon as she found out and I believe she is now in the Med with her parents. All the money any of us has – except for my husband of course – has been frozen. Meanwhile, my husband has disappeared with my children." I spat breathlessly, seething. "I would say that was enough to tip anyone over the edge, wouldn't you?" My vitriol was evident, but I was beyond caring.

"I see," said the officer, embarrassed.

"You say your children are missing?" he officer who, until now, had remained quiet, questioned.

"That's right, but technically they're on holiday with their father." I decided to say nothing more. I didn't feel I could trust anybody anymore and I wasn't convinced the police would help my search; they could even hinder it and I couldn't deal with that.

"Do you think they're in any danger?" the same officer asked.

"It would be easier if I could say their father was unstable and incapable of taking care of them, but no, Mike adores our daughters. I know they're fine with him, for the moment." My voice began to falter. "But they should be here with me," I couldn't help adding.

"You obviously know the police can't get involved in a situation like this if the children aren't considered to be in any danger. Even if he is being investigated. As long as there's no warrant out for his arrest, we can't stop him from taking his children on holiday."

"Officer, do you think I'm stupid? I know that, I also know that once they're in America – which is where I believe they have gone – they can stay there for up to three months, legally." I was tired, stressed and thoroughly miserable; I just wanted these people out of my home. The policemen must have sensed my mood and stood to leave.

"If you think circumstances have changed, and you feel the police may be able to help, then please do contact us," offered the younger officer.

As I opened the front door to the freezing weather and said goodbye to the police officers, I knew I had been somewhat short, even rude, but didn't much care.

With the letter in my hand, I returned to my stool in the kitchen, it apparently having become my permanent perch. I sat in the dusky half-light which comes with a winter morning, wondering how Marcia had taken the news of Alex's death. Poor Alex, he had been so sensitive; Marcia was his everything, he would have done anything for her. His world had been turned upside down by someone he loved and trusted, and they had betrayed him. I felt guilty for not having taken more notice of him, wrapped up as I was in my own problems. We had all failed him, but Mike most of all. I made a vow to make sure justice would be done for Alex, and for myself, his death crystallizing my resolve.

I turned the envelope over and over in my hands before finally opening it. The note was short. In it, Alex apologised for not noticing anything untoward going on at the firm and further apologised for not being strong enough to be there for me. It ended with a wish that his godchildren and I were reunited and, perhaps surprisingly, that nothing too awful happened to Mike. I was drained, emotionally and physically, and placed the note back into the envelope. I fought back the sensation of drowning; air was being forced from my lungs, the weight of all that had happened seeming almost too much to bear. I gave myself a moment to re-group; I had more pressing matters.

I checked the kitchen clock, and upon deciding there was no point going back to bed, I started to prepare for the day ahead. A twinge of excitement rose whenever I thought what could happen today if all went according to plan, yet I fought back the feelings of hope, trying desperately to prepare myself for disappointment. My thoughts and emotions were exhausting me, the tumultuous swinging from positive to negative taking its toll. After numerous cups of coffee and a forced slice of toast, it was time to leave for the building society.

On the way, I placed a call to the travel agents to check availability for an evening flight to Orlando that day. Fortunately, there was plenty of availability. With the price confirmed, I reserved a seat on the flight and arranged to go to their offices later with payment. The ticket would be issued on departure due to the lateness of the booking. Once more, I prayed all this speculation about the savings account hadn't been in vain.

I experienced a perverse excitement upon entering the building society, feeling as if I were committing a crime. I knew this wasn't true; the money, if it was there, did belong to me. However, I was guilty of not being entirely honest by using my maiden name, which I wasn't legally allowed to do. Standing in the queue and waiting my turn, I gently drummed my fingers on the cover of the savings book, allowing my mind to wander a moment.

The building society was one of the smaller, independent ones who still operated in an almost old-fashioned way. They had computerised systems like the rest of the world, but business could often be conducted without so many of the strict guidelines, using a more personal touch than the larger financial institutions.

When it was finally my turn to be seen, I almost forgot what I was doing and was about to announce myself as Mrs Weston. Checking myself just in time, I struck up an animated conversation about holidays, flights, jetlag, anything that kept the cashier talking. I passed the savings book under the clear security screen to her and requested the book be updated. No comment was made as to the amount of time elapsed since the book was last presented. I guessed it must not be uncommon for some of the society's customers to be long term investors, happy to leave funds untouched.

I hid my relief and the tears that sprang to my eyes when I saw there was money in the account, as well as the utter delight at the amount of interest it had accrued over the years. I now had a little over four thousand pounds. With some irony, I smiled; this small sum now felt like a king's ransom. In what I now regarded as my old life, it could have represented the bill for a weekend away and a small shopping trip. Now, it meant a chance to find my children.

I asked the cashier for a cheque to be drawn and gave the travel agent's details, then, almost as an afterthought, asked if it might be possible to withdraw a thousand pounds in cash. The cashier had to leave the counter with the book to clear the request with her supervisor, explaining that with the amount being over the maximum daily amount, as well as it being such short notice, authorization would be needed.

It seemed like a lifetime passed – in reality, it was only a couple of minutes – before the cashier reappeared, saying that my withdrawal had been approved. She did, however, ask that in the future, I bear in mind the society's rules regarding cash withdrawals. I apologised profusely and promised to give sufficient notice next time. Thanking the cashier again, I left the building society and hurried down the street to the travel agents, with the first genuine smile in what seemed like an eternity spread across my face. I felt I was getting some good luck at last.

At the travel agency, I was asked if I had any special requirements for meals during the flight and the usual check-in details were given. With the reference number safely tucked in my passport, which was also checked for validity, I was all set. I had to be at the airport at least three hours before take-off, which only left me five hours to pack and find somewhere to store any furniture I was hoping to keep. Unfortunately, there would be no time for me to organise somewhere to live – that would have to be dealt with on my return. Perhaps a cheap hotel stay would have to initially suffice.

I realised that in the space of forty-eight hours my life had been reduced to anything I could stuff into a few boxes and bags. Everything else would have to wait. Finding solace in the flight reservation details I now held close, and the money safely in my wallet, I buttoned up my coat and turned up the collar as I once again turned onto the high street where the wind was blowing in biting gusts. I felt a new strength and more hope than I had ever thought possible.

Letting myself into the comfort of my car, I was grateful for the blast of heat from the internal system. I realised I didn't know if the car had been included in the financial freeze by the tax officials but didn't really care; if they could find it, they could have it. I laughed out loud to myself as to how mercenary I had suddenly become.

8.

Driving home, I made a mental note of things I could pack in boxes for my return, and what clothes I would take for the trip. Mike's mobile phone, which I guessed must be under another name as it was still working, was now fully charged and I placed a call to the family solicitors. I desperately needed to speak to them regarding the house, still unable to believe it had been sold. The solicitors were a firm that had been used by both Mike and I over the years, mainly for the writing of wills and general advice. Patiently, I waited to be connected to Mr Pickering, whom I had spoken to in the past, but not for some time.

Mr Pickering eventually came onto the line and I instantly sensed there was something wrong. His tone was one of a parent trying to placate a distraught child. When questioned about the house sale, there was something in his clipped answers that suggested he had been warned I might call and what best to say to me.

I had no idea what Mike had told the solicitor, but it was clear I wouldn't be able to achieve anything. Time was in too short supply to dwell on my conversation, or lack thereof, with the solicitor, so I finished the call and moved onto the next task. Pulling away into the light traffic, the rain began to fall again. Now, my mind was thinking of sunnier climes and what my next move might be when I got to America.

Back at the house, which now felt cold and uninviting, I moved quickly from room to room, making a list of small yet valuable items; things I could sell if I had to. Silverware, figurines, jewellery, first edition books, small paintings, these were items that could be used for income upon my return. I had decided Phoebe and Alice could return to boarding at their school while I arranged for somewhere to live.

Money would be a great concern, having not worried about it in a long time, as would finding a job, which I knew I would have to do. Once again, I forced myself to concentrate on matters of immediate importance.

Packing my boxes of valuables into the boot and squeezing some of the children's clothes into the corners, along with any other available space, I was beginning to feel I was making progress. The boot was completely full within an hour. If I was going to have to leave the car somewhere so conspicuous as the airport, I didn't want any of the contents to be readily seen – so when the boot was full, that was the limit. Covering everything with a couple of blankets, I closed and locked the car.

A trip to Perse School was the next thing on my agenda. I thought it would be a good idea to inform Mrs Anderson of the latest developments and to let her know of my impending trip. Drawing up to the familiar gate, I felt the now common pang of sorrow from the heart-wrenching need to hold my children.

The headmistress greeted me with an open smile. I wondered if she could see the defiance in my eyes; I was fighting back. I told her of my plans as we made our way to her office. We discussed the possibility of Phoebe and Alice boarding at the school on their return with there being no family home, wanting as normal a life as possible for them to return to.

"I understand the fees will need to be increased and, as I am sure you are aware by now, I have no means of supporting myself but I do hope to rectify that when I get home." It felt better having made the request. Mrs Anderson could only say yes or no now.

"Mrs Weston, in light of recent events and how I have come to know you, the school would be delighted to have your girls board with us for as long as is necessary. It does, however, cause me some concern as to the arrangements you have made for yourself." She paused for a moment and then added, "Our caretaker is due to retire very shortly and the position needs to be filled. The duties are to oversee the cleaning, gardening and maintenance of the school. The real advantage of this though, is that there's accommodation with the position. I would like to offer you the post but would ask that you do not make an immediate decision – just bear the offer in mind for your return."

Being overwhelmed by the generosity and kindness of the woman standing in front of me, I could only smile in reply and lunged forward to hug her, trying desperately to contain the tears of gratitude. When I let her go, I instantly felt foolish and embarrassed, but was pleased to see that she was smiling at me.

She continued, "Furthermore, should you decide you don't want to take the position, you are more than welcome to come and stay as guests at my home until you find yourself settled." I couldn't believe my luck; the open and kind nature of this woman standing opposite me had instilled a feeling of hope and support within me.

"Mrs. Anderson, how can I ever thank you?" was all I could muster.

"By you and your children returning safe and well."

"I can assure you that is my sole intention." If she knew anything about the business affairs or what had surely already been printed in local papers, she didn't let on. I was grateful for her discretion.

Mrs Anderson regarded me for a moment, then asked a question that I had a feeling had been on her mind for some time.

"You don't feel your children are in any danger, yet you're going to travel thousands of miles in the hope of bringing them home?"

"I know their father loves them dearly, but he has done things that will tear their world apart. I don't think they're aware of anything yet, and when the time comes for them to know, it's going to be very hard for them." I paused for a moment keeping my composure in check. "Mike may even have to go to prison for his deeds and I want them be involved as little as possible. It's my job as their mother to protect them, and I can only do that when I have them here with me. I have an idea where they are, but that could change in the blink of an eye. I can't take that risk; they should be home with me." I needed to get on with other matters in preparation for my trip and thanked the headmistress again for her help, feeling as though an unlikely and precious friendship had been born.

"You are a remarkable woman and I wish you the very best of luck. I have no doubt you'll be successful; I look forward to seeing you and your daughters very soon."

I left, emotional, with a renewed sense of hope.

There was little more than two hours before I had to be at the airport. I made some last-minute checks: money, passport and tickets. The small bag I had packed hardly seemed enough for the trip, but I needed to travel light – there would be no evenings out, no need to change for dinner. Checking my ticket again, I marvelled at my luck, having been able to book a seat coming home on the same return flight as Mike. There would be no extra expense of trying to change tickets or departure dates should luck be shining on me, and my hunch prove to be right.

***

After driving around the airport car park a few times, I decided on a parking spot between a Range Rover and a VW Golf, right in the middle of the busy car park. I hoped my car would be overlooked amongst the hundreds of cars there – I doubted it, but it was a risk I had to take. Locking the car and setting the alarm, I walked swiftly towards the terminal building, offering up a small prayer that the car would still be there when I returned.

It was getting dark as I made my way across the car park. It surprised me just how many people there were milling around, getting in and out of cars and coaches. Groups of people waited to collect luggage from the under-floor storage lockers which opened automatically when passengers disembarked from the coaches, then threw them onto trolleys.

Finding the correct check-in queue, I waited in line with the other holidaymakers, careful to avoid eye-contact. The last thing I wanted was to have to make conversation with strangers, too much needed to be planned. I pretended to be engrossed in texting, going in and out of Mike's phone options. His menus were standard, and I was surprised at how little there was in his message inbox. There were only half a dozen messages from a 'B Office' whoever that was, guessing someone from work. As I scrolled down, it became obvious they were replies to whatever messages Mike had sent. The last one read, 'room booked at usual hotel, see you there'. It was from months ago. I decided to dismiss the issue, concluding my mind was occupied enough with recent events. The sent box was empty, as were all the other menus, any information I might have gathered was long gone. I turned off the phone in preparation for boarding my flight.

Once the boarding pass was issued and bags tagged and dumped unceremoniously on the moving conveyor belt, there was time to think. Stealing myself to a quiet corner, I began to plan. I knew from what little the travel agent had divulged that there had only been one night's accommodation booked through them. The ten-day package, which included flight, car, one night's hotel stay and Disney passes, hadn't been upgraded in any way.

I didn't know Florida at all and wasn't hugely confident about having to travel around it on my own. I prayed Mike and my children stayed close to the theme parks, though even this offered me no consolation. I knew how vast everything in America was; luck would need to be shining on me for the next week or so. My biggest fear was that Mike might get adventurous and take the children all over Florida, or further afield.

After browsing through the airport shops, visiting each one at least twice and drinking three cups of coffee, the announcement to board the aircraft came. I held back from the other holidaymakers and watched, with mounting despair, as excited children dragged their parents closer to the boarding gates, desperate to get on the plane as if hurrying the process would make the aircraft take off sooner.

Teenagers the same age as my own lounged around, pretending to be ultra-cool and unaffected by the whole process. Everyone else seemed full of excitement and enthusiasm for their trip. My trip was for an entirely different reason, one of searching and then getting my girls home with me – hopefully with as little fuss as possible. I had to try and come up with a plan as to how I was going fulfil my goals and get my children back.

***

Beth Sweeney had been a flight attendant, as ground crew, for almost ten years and had experienced, or seen, almost every type of passenger and traveller there was to see, from high-flying businessmen and celebrities, to hundreds of thousands of holidaymakers. She had noticed the woman wandering around the departure lounge.

People watching, even after all the years, was still one of her favourite pastimes; it was one of the reasons she had loved her job for so long, never wanting to change her career. There were always children crying, and over-excited youngsters running around, no matter the time of year, though it was never quite as prolific as in the height of the season when all the schools were on holiday. At that time of year, you barely noticed the faces as they skimmed past you in droves.

This lady stood out. It was obvious before long that she was travelling on her own, having had a few coffees alone in the café and never striking up conversation with anyone. She held back from the crowds gathering to board the plane, preferring to stay on the outskirts of the mass of people, all now jostling for the boarding passes to be stamped and allowed to board the plane. As Beth worked through the groups, she noticed economy class was filling up rapidly with almost all passengers boarded.

Eventually, the woman came closer. She had a worried look on her face and kept rubbing her forehead as if trying to stave off an impending headache. Yes, the more Beth studied the woman, the more she felt her trip was not one of frivolity and pleasure. Beth noticed the dark circles around her eyes that no amount of make-up could hide, and she was dressed immaculately in colour coordinated linen trousers and jacket. She wore an expensive watch – one that Beth had thought about purchasing herself, but had never been able to warrant the expenditure – and had the latest fashionable sunglasses perched on her head. She had the effortless look of someone who had money and natural style. Beth guessed she was probably booked into business class or first class.

Finally, it was the woman's turn in the queue. As she handed over her boarding pass, Beth immediately noticed it was an economy ticket. She was a little surprised and, in an instant, made her decision. With one glance, she checked the manifest for the flight; economy showed as being almost full to capacity, but there were plenty of available seats in business class. Today, this sad and worried looking lady would have at least one thing to smile about.

***

As the announcer called the last request for my flight, I reached the front of the queue. I stepped forward and gave my passport and boarding pass to the glamorous looking girl at the boarding desk.

"Travelling alone, madam?" The question startled me, and I was instantly suspicious.

"Yes, that right," I said, striking a defensive tone. What business was it of this woman anyway?

"Would madam care to join our business class passengers?" Not waiting for a reply, the stunning air stewardess continued, "Turn left at the end of the walkway and someone will show you to your seat."

I was dumbstruck, looking up as she passed me my ticket. She smiled, adding with a reassuring look, "With compliments of the airline."

"Thank you very much," I spluttered, trying to regain my composure as I accepted the offer, reprimanding myself for being so rude. And so began the first leg of my journey – maybe an impromptu upgrade was a sign of good things to come; I certainly hoped so.

Settling into the oversized, and extremely comfortable, pod seat, I was suddenly aware of just how tired I was. My eyes grew heavy as take-off began and I felt exhaustion flow through me. Thinking of the past, there was a time I had always flown first class, accompanying Mike so much that, at one point, I had almost become his personal assistant – much to the annoyance of his actual personal assistant. Little did I know that our spending time together would diminish so drastically, and with such disastrous consequences.

9.

It felt like an eternity, but slowly the eight-hour flight passed. I'd slept for some of it but was dogged by terrible dreams of lost children crying, followed by the subsequent feeling of helplessness. I could see them but couldn't reach them, our fingers just too far apart to touch. If only I could touch them, I knew I could help. Waking with tears streaming down my face, the need to vomit was almost overwhelming, I had to stop myself retching with the physical pain of my loss. I knew I couldn't stand any more of the dreams. Reaching into my pocket, I felt the familiar picture I carried of Alice and Phoebe, but was unable to bring myself to look at it for fear of emotions overwhelming me again; instead, I took comfort in just knowing it was there. It was taken only a few weeks ago, a simple shot of my two young girls laughing together, enjoying life. This photo now felt like the most precious item in the world and touching it made me feel a little closer to them, reminding me why I was even attempting the trip.

Turning on an in-flight movie, I didn't bother following the plot – I was just grateful for the distraction from my mind, fighting back the fear I may never see my children again. The questions came again; was this trip for nothing? What possible hope did I have of finding them, least of all in America? Had I engineered the situation? Reading too much into very little evidence, thereby creating something that doesn't exist?

Head hurting, I ordered a double scotch; maybe alcohol would relax me. If nothing else, it gave me something else to do. Sitting on the plane didn't feel constructive in any way, and I began to watch the clock in the corner of screen, counting away the minutes. The scotch relaxed my limbs but did nothing for my mind.

I had two more drinks in quick succession – they must have had some effect, as I felt the fog of sleep descend again and I was grateful for its oblivion. The gentle shaking of my shoulder brought me out of slumber; the flight attendant was asking me to fasten my seat belt, flight almost over.

As we came in to land, I allowed the other passengers to disembark first. I tried to regain my composure and formulate a simple plan of action once off the aircraft. I decided all I could do was make my way to the hotel where Mike had been booked in for the first night and take things from there.

My initial inclination was to hire a car upon arrival, but I changed my mind as soon as I landed. I didn't feel capable of concentrating on new road signs, nor driving on the opposite side of the road, especially in a car I wasn't familiar with. After a few helpfully answered questions from the airport and airline staff, I boarded the coach for the hotel with ease. Bouncing along with all the other passengers and staring in awe at the array of shops, motels, hotels and restaurants on the journey, I congratulated myself on my choice; much better to let someone else take the strain. There was also an opportunity to think and adjust to my surroundings without interruption.

The hotel, like most others I had seen on the short journey, was huge, though I was slightly taken aback as to its simplicity. Mike had always stayed in first-class accommodation, enjoying the finest dining and amenities; this hotel, on the other hand, was more along the lines of being 'excellent value for money' – not a phrase I would associate with my husband's usual choice of anything. I consciously attempted to not dwell on this, it only lending itself to more doubt as to my being there in the first place. Having studied the brochure I had found, I knew there were over a thousand rooms, divided between three huge blocks.

After checking in, a porter carried my single bag to my room and provided a quick run-through of all the facilities the hotel had to offer. Even in the evening, the heat was relentless, but the warmth on my skin soothed me.

Feeling for the picture of my girls again, I thought I should go straight to reception and start asking questions; perhaps seeing if there was a reservation for Mike. Maybe someone had seen the girls – should I stop people and show them the photo of Alice and Phoebe? Taking a deep breath, I realised I was becoming increasingly anxious and probably wasn't in the right frame of mind to be approaching innocent people on their holidays – someone would likely call security if there was a stranger badgering people randomly in the foyer. I had to think smart; there was no point sabotaging my own efforts. The best idea would probably be to settle into my room, take a shower and take stock of things.

I didn't feel I should unpack too much – jetlag was starting to set in and I was a bit unsettled, making any form of decisiveness difficult. A quick shower and change of clothes later, I felt slightly more positive and wanted to begin my search. With the picture in my jeans pocket, I left the room to explore a little. The bright lights of the main building seemed to spread across the whole hotel. Figuring this was as good a place to start as any, I picked my way around the moist lawns, sprinkler systems working over-time in the dusk.

As I stood at the reception desk, I scoured the lobby for familiar faces, wanting each child I saw to be my own. There was a small queue of people in front of me, waiting to check-in, so I was able to get a good look around whilst waiting my turn. There was a restaurant to the right of reception, coffee shop to the left. Even though it was obvious everyone waiting had just arrived, cases in tow and sporting the dishevelled look travelling can often bestow, I strained my ears trying to eavesdrop on conversations hoping I'd overhear something;

perhaps a snippet of useful information, or a casual remark that might be valuable to me in some way.

Because I had no room number for Mike, or any other information relating to their booking, the hotel was unable to confirm or deny if the party was still registered at the hotel. I wasn't a member of the party and hotel policy meant no information could be divulged. I didn't want to leave a message – it would tip off Mike I was in America, and I couldn't risk what he might do if he knew I was here. I felt no one wanted to help me. My maternal instinct was urging me again to thrust the picture of Phoebe and Alice in front of every person I saw, begging them to tell me if they had seen my children, and bombard hotel staff with questions, demanding they give me information but what good would that have done?

If I made a nuisance of myself, I would likely end up thrown out of the hotel, the only place I had any idea Mike and girls may have been. At a complete loss as to what to do next, I left the main building. I returned to my room, consumed by hopelessness at the enormity of my plight. Laying in the darkness, listening to the loud hum of the air-conditioning unit, there was even more time to think. Over the last couple of days my mind had been only focused on getting my daughters back with me and home safely; I hadn't addressed my feelings toward Mike in any detail. He had become an object – no longer my husband, but my opponent, someone who had stolen from me and deceived me.

Now that there was an opportunity to think about us, I wasn't sure I wanted to. I didn't have the energy.

Did I hate him? Did I love him? What happened between us that made everything go so wrong, and when? A hundred questions remained unanswered. He had become a stranger in such a short time and it was a mystery as to how I would react when I saw him again.

Feeling unhinged and not knowing what to do next, I couldn't stop the tears falling and gave in to the hopelessness I felt. There was no one here; no one to comfort me, to seek solace with, no one I could even call for advice. Eventually the tears slowed, my mind a hazy fog. I recognised just how exhausted I was and as I laid on the bed, trying to consider my next move, I unwittingly drifted into sleep. The nightmares came again, and again. Each time I was about to touch my children, rescuing them, their images faded away, leaving me bereft. Waking once more, sobbing uncontrollably, I felt I might die from the pain in my heart that would only be eased by finding my babies. I didn't know how much more I could take.

By six am, local time, I had been awake for hours, my body clock shattered. Having had some sleep, albeit disturbed, I was able to think a little more clearly. The sun was already beating down, and through the window I could see it was set to be another bright day.

The one element I was certain of was Mike's love for our children. He would in no way deliberately hurt them, but hadn't he already done that with his actions? For hours, I laid on the hard mattress trying to think logically about how to move forward in my search until it was almost lunchtime. My jetlag and anxiety had robbed me of any normality to mealtimes. I wasn't hungry, but knew without food, I was no good to anyone.

Questions as to how to proceed were buzzing around my head; should I attempt to search the theme parks, or should I wait in the hotel? There was also the ever-present threat that they may have moved on. Pushing the thought from my mind, I hoped Alice and Phoebe would remain true to form and want to stay where the greatest concentration of shops and amusements were.

I decided that a day at the hotel may be a good idea due to the amount of time already elapsed. There was always the chance I may find out something useful, but if I was going to stay at the hotel, the aim had to be to confirm my family were still staying here.

The restaurant was serving a lunchtime buffet and I seized the opportunity to take as long as possible over the meal, hungry or not. The seating arrangements were such that some tables were laid for two, some for four or six, with long tables down the centre of the room for larger parties who wished to sit together. Courses comprised a soup or salad for starter, beef casserole or chicken curry for main course and at least six different choices for dessert. Fruit, cheese and biscuits were also on offer.

I barely took any notice of what starter I chose and found myself a table for two, as far away as possible from the main bulk of people. I acknowledged that inviting myself onto a table seating a larger group may make it easier to gather information, but I knew I wasn't ready to be the 'gregarious traveller' quite yet. Too little sleep and too much worry had seen to that. Convincing myself that watching and listening would be just as productive, I settled myself at the small table.

The dining room began to fill, and within twenty minutes there were four or five families noisily deciding what to eat. Some staff, obviously on their lunch break, made their way to the corner of the room that appeared to be their usual spot. Children were running around, deciding to sit one place, then two minutes later changing their minds. With all the commotion, nobody paid any attention to the quiet lady sitting on her own in the corner and I was able to watch without disturbance.

Taking my starter plate back untouched, I slipped the contents into the bin as I passed. When I thought enough time had passed, I left the table for another course and made sure to take the longest route to the buffet, weaving through almost half the tables in the room, trying to absorb every detail, overhear every word.

I watched a large group of holiday reps make their way into the room. It was then that I had an idea; I could pose as someone who was interested in becoming a holiday rep – I might be able to gain the confidence of some of them with my questions about the job and, hopefully, get some useful information. I decided I would be fairly recently divorced, which would account for my being alone and looking for a career change. The story began to expand in my mind; if it was kept simple, it might just work.

Disregarding the fact I was mentally and physically exhausted, I waited until the group had made their meal choices and sat down, then went over to the table. I could feel myself trembling with nerves, knowing I had to try to keep it together. To make my story convincing, I would have to appear outgoing, confident and willing to listen. As I approached, I saw two of the female members of the group were from my own travel company, their badges clearly displaying the company name in bright red lettering above their own.

It was comforting to see a few appear to be about the same age as me; I had wondered initially if I may be viewed as being too old for such a position. Gathering all the courage I could muster, I addressed the group with a sunny smile.

"Would you mind if I joined you?" I let my eyes fall on each person in turn, smile frozen on my face. I could feel a flush rising from my neck and knew I was reddening.

"Not at all," replied a male from the party. It was a start, but I knew my explanation for wanting to join them would have to be given quickly lest I be regarded as one of life's many misfits and discounted before I had even begun.

Introducing myself as visiting family in the area, I told them of my interest in a career change, explaining I had been considering tourism and that I would appreciate an insight into the duties and responsibilities of their work. The story appeared to go down well with my audience, and it wasn't long before I felt reasonably confident and relaxed a little. A couple of the group were less keen to open up as the rest, so I decided to concentrate on the people I was sitting closest to.

There was one man who was very friendly and wanted to chat; he could later prove useful and I encouraged him to talk. The lady to my right happily introduced herself as Tilly, and before long she had confided that she was also divorced which had helped her decision to become a travel rep. Feeling there was a common link between us, Tilly went on to tell more about herself. Encouragingly, she was a little older than me, though she certainly didn't look it, and I felt a little more credibility was added to my plan.

Tilly was happy to chat about clients and the job; it transpired there were four companies represented at the table and she went on to explain that they all knew each other, having worked this particular destination for some time now. If one of them needed cover or had other business to attend to, as was occasionally the case, they helped each other out. I was surprised at how interesting the role seemed and got a good insight into how travellers' needs were met.

I felt I was now brave enough to ask the question I had been desperate to know the answer to ever since the idea had first come to me.

"If, for example, you had a party on a fly-drive holiday and you had to contact them for some reason, how could you do that?" I tried to sound casual , addressing the group as a whole, though some were now involved in their own paperwork and discussions. Fortunately, Tilly answered enthusiastically.

"We have a manifest for each departure date at both ends of the holiday. For example, you left the UK on…?" I gave my departure date as the one Mike and the girls had travelled.

"Right, the 11th from Gatwick, which meant you arrived on the 12th at Orlando. My manifest would show your name…?" she trailed suggestively, gesturing for my surname.

"Mrs Weston, Julia,'" I blurted out quickly.

"So, my manifest sheet would have your name and departure date from the UK for the 11th, as well as the arrival date in the US. It would also have your departure date from the US and arrival date in the UK," Tilly explained, seemingly enjoying the attention. "There would be other information on the manifest too, such as hotel, special requirements – that sort of thing."

I deliberately looked a little confused, hoping to spur things on.

"I could show you, if you like." Tilly was already reaching for her huge bag and pulling out a thick sheaf of papers. My heart leapt and I tried to look coolly interested, rather than frantically excited. I tried to slow the pounding in my chest as Tilly went through her papers.

Finally, Tilly found what she was looking for and spread some papers on the table. She then went through, from start to finish, all the information contained in the manifest. She produced three, all dated for the last few days of the current month. Perplexed, Tilly tried to find my details on the manifest for the 11th & 12th, until, in a fit of mock absentmindedness and a shower of apologies, I explained my original plans for travel were for the 11th but I had to settle for the 12th. This meant my arrival would have been the 13th. Armed with the correct information, Tilly promptly found the correct entry, satisfied that all was in order before offering to go and get coffee. The rest of the group was beginning to disperse, returning to the day's tasks. I took my chance as Tilly wound her way to the coffee bar.

I discreetly studied the manifest dated 11th and 12th and saw an entry for Mike; it confirmed there was a one-night booking at the Quality Inn Plaza but contained no further accommodation details.

10.

Tilly explained that fly-drive holidays were the hardest to keep track of because the client had no obligation to inform the tour operator of their whereabouts, though it made good sense in case there was cause for them to be contacted. The visa requirements dictated you had to provide the first night's accommodation so that US Immigration had some record of travel, but there was no need to provide any further information.

A little subdued, I was now none the wiser as to where Mike or my children were. Tilly returned with the coffees.

"When did you decide you might want to work in the travel industry, become a rep?"

"Not too long ago," I hedged, deliberately evasive.

"It's not always a blast, but most of the time it sure beats sitting at a desk, typing letters all day for a living."

I didn't want to say that I doubted I had the ability to even do that.

"Long haul is usually the best deal because people tend to have a pretty good idea of what they want to do when they get to their destination. They have, in most cases, spent a lot of money and want to make the most of it," she added, before looking at her watch. "I'm afraid it's my turn to sell the theme park passes – it's probably the most hated job, but the commission isn't bad. Do you fancy meeting for a bite to eat later? It's nice to chat to someone of similar years, if you know what I mean. You may have noticed most of us are in the twenty-something bracket." She laughed, adding in a whisper, "The rest of us are considered dinosaurs."

"That would be great, thanks for the insight," I smiled.

"Glad to help. Oh, just one more thing; the manifests are supposed to be confidential."

"Message received and understood – my lips are sealed." I mock saluted my new friend as she gathered up her belongings and disappeared into the packed lobby. Before parting company, we'd agreed to meet for seven that evening and I was surprised at how much my spirits had lifted at the thought of our dinner date, though I still felt incapable of eating. Information about my family was all I hungered for and trying to act upbeat and charming had proven exhausting too.

Alone again, a wave of panic and doubt engulfed me once more; what if I was putting too much emphasis on the hotel? If they weren't here, I was wasting valuable time talking to people, stupidly arranging dinner dates, and for what? That being said, what else was I going to do? I couldn't spend time travelling aimlessly all over Florida on the off chance I catch a glimpse of my children. No matter how immense the task was, I had to remain calm and at least form some sort of connection to the area and the people in it.

In some ways, I felt guilty for not telling Tilly the truth, but I couldn't risk it; I needed to be confident and focused. If I told someone the whole story, particularly someone I had only just met, it could ruin everything. I might not be believed, or worse, be seen as some sort of weirdo and have the authorities called.

I spent a little more time at the restaurant, lingering over my cold, stagnant coffee. I didn't know what my reaction would be should I see Mike, and I felt totally out of control. By now, there were very few people left in the dining area and I felt there was nothing more to be gained being there.

Jetlag was playing havoc with my body clock, so I decided to try and get some more sleep, not caring it was ill-advised. There was nothing more I could do right now – nothing that would help anyway. Stepping out into the warm sunshine, I made my way back to my room. Regardless of what happened, I hoped my children were enjoying themselves in the sun. Taking a shower and getting changed, I set my alarm for six and climbed into bed.

***

I woke with a start, alarm blaring. For a split-second, I thought it was the beginning of an ordinary day at home before my mind caught up, and the heavy weight of depression descended. I remembered the dinner date that had been arranged with Tilly; I really wasn't in the mood. What was the point? I shouldn't be gallivanting around whilst my children were lost god knows where. Though I had to admit, as much as I didn't want to, that I needed help; I couldn't do this alone. I now knew people who worked in the area and, right now, it was my only option.

Eventually, I swung my legs out of the huge bed. Another shower and I was pulling on a pair of lightweight trousers and a clean shirt. From what I had seen so far, nobody dressed up for dinner – or any other meal for that matter. With my limited resources, I was rather thankful for this.

Tilly was waiting at the front of the hotel and it was comforting to see a friendly face amongst the hundreds of strangers. I had never felt as alone as I did on arriving in Orlando; all the other travellers had appeared to know where they were going, what they were doing. Nobody had looked like me, a fish out of water.

"I thought we might go out of town a little," suggested Tilly as we hugged.

"I don't have a car," I said, suddenly embarrassed by my own inadequacy.

She laughed. "I know you don't have a car, silly, but I do. One of the perks of the job when on long haul

– you get a car for the duration. Great for shopping and nights like this."

"That's another good point to add to my list!" I added, remembering my story to Tilly and trying to sound upbeat.

We drove a short way on the main highway and then took an exit out to the next town or suburb; I wasn't sure which. It appeared to me that American towns seemed to sprawl across vast areas, not always having a real centre, so you were never quite sure if you were still in the same town or a new one. We chatted easily about mundane, everyday topics and I began to relax a little, grateful for somebody else driving. It was one less thing to think about.

Another ten minutes and we pulled into the large car park of what was clearly a Chinese restaurant. It was built to replicate an authentic Chinese temple; emerald green walls, a golden tiled roof and two large, bright red dragons winding themselves up the supporting pillars of the entrance completing the effect. Somehow, none of this seemed out of place here; the more outrageous, the better.

I ordered beef in black bean sauce and a beer; I wasn't hungry but could gladly do with a drink. Tilly, after much deliberation, settled on the same. My companion was an easy talker and had no difficulty in opening up. She told how she married young and, almost from the start, knew it had been a mistake. Never having lived together in anything other than small, beaten up trailers, he was a vicious drunk and spent any money she earned on booze. His temper resulted in him beating her, all the while throwing out callous accusations of her being lazy, useless and fat.

The jobs she'd held previously were usually twelve-hour shifts in petrol stations or waitressing for a number of strip clubs; when he started getting physically violent, she finally left him. She explained that there comes a time when your mind finally clears of the fog and the solution becomes clear. Alcoholics or substance abusers often refer to it as 'a moment of clarity', which she said was ironic, taking a slug from her beer bottle and laughing, as until that point she didn't really drink.

As if reading my mind, she went on to say that, after her experience, there had been no need of a permanent replacement in her life. In fact, now, it would probably only complicate matters. She also enjoyed the freedom of not having to answer to anyone but herself. I could see that Tilly was waiting for me to respond with my own story; fear and panic began to rise. Would now be a good time to tell the truth? I felt she could keep a secret and would be sympathetic to my dilemma, but I still decided against it, feeling it was too soon.

There would come a point when I would tell the truth, everything from the start, but for now I decided it was best to keep my friend in the dark.

Tilly was still waiting for a reply to her question about my own story, gently running her fingers around the rim of her bottle. As if on cue, a costume-clad waiter appeared with our food. Knowing I couldn't stall any longer, I made up a simple storyline for myself, telling how my husband had ran off with another woman and left me with nothing except a few personal savings, just enough to start a new life. This, I felt, was not a million miles from the truth and I hoped it sounded convincing. Tilly listened and murmured empathetic comments, along with the offer to help me as much as possible.

She promised she would make enquiries within her own company to see if there were any positions available, and in the meantime was happy to give me as much information as possible. She claimed to have given herself the mission of sending me home with the knowledge of exactly what a travel rep's job entailed, enough insight that would, at the very least, grant me the possibility of employment. I was filled with gratitude and guilt. Never had I met someone who wanted to genuinely put themselves out on my account. I realised I had never really had a true friend, not knowing what one was until now.

My mind drifted back to when Marcia and I were younger. We had been best friends, been at college together, but ultimately, Marcia only ever looked out for one person – Marcia. As long as she was okay, then anything and anyone else, wasn't her concern. I acknowledged the painful reality that Marcia hadn't even attempted to contact me since that fateful day when life had changed forever.

I wondered just how upset she was about Alex's death. Likely, she would have been embarrassed by the scandal of Alex having taken his own life, rather than giving a thought as to the reasons why. Poor Alex; my heart went out to him. My own life had been turned upside down, but Alex's had been utterly destroyed.

I was suddenly aware I had been staring blankly for too long and apologised to Tilly for being such lousy company. She wouldn't hear of it and together we turned the conversation to happier things. We talked about clothes, money and how wonderful it would be to live in the sunshine all year round. I felt like I was acting, not myself at all, but I knew it was for a good cause. I decided not to mention my children; I would leave that for another time. Tilly may have thought it odd for me to be considering a career that required large amounts of travel when I had children to consider. It was far simpler to be divorced with no strings attached.

It was dark when we left the restaurant and we both realised how long we had spent over our meal. True, we had gone on to have three coffees, two of which I had let go cold, and a dessert, again, untouched by me. I was beginning to feel more comfortable in her company and, when I was dropped off outside my room, I felt fortunate that I had found such a friend, and thanked her profusely for the evening.

Tilly said we could catch up at some point the following day, but it would most likely be in the late afternoon or early evening as she had a new party of holidaymakers due at midday which took some time to organise. We said goodnight and I let myself into the cool bedroom, tired and still wondering if I was doing the right thing, making the right decisions. I was no further along but I was desperately trying to stay optimistic.

Slowly, a plan began to formulate in my mind as I was undressing, and I would put it into play the following morning. My head hit the pillow and I succumbed to sleep within minutes – thankfully there were no dreams this time.

My day dawned to the rhythmic drumming of heavy rain against tarmac, and the air in the room felt damp. I talked myself into getting out of bed, and it was then that I realised the room was quieter than normal. I couldn't hear the usual humming of my air-conditioning unit and, after a quick check, I concluded it wasn't working, the dampness I felt was humidity. Peeking out through the curtains, I saw the rain hitting the hot tarmac, causing a steamy mist to linger above the roads and pavements.

After a shower, I dressed and went to the hotel restaurant for the breakfast buffet. Although not hungry, as always I told myself I had to eat something. My main reason for going to the restaurant was to see if Tilly was around – my plan would only work if she wasn't in the vicinity.

The dining area was packed with people and there seemed to be more children on the rampage than the previous day. My eyes scanned the room, taking in the multi-coloured Hawaiian shirts that seemed to be standard issue for men on holiday. I still looked at the children as if each might be mine, regardless of age or sex; I wondered if I was beginning to lose my mind. I couldn't see Tilly, nor any of the other representatives.

Checking my watch and seeing it was nine thirty, I decided I would have something to eat and then occupy myself in the gift shop until around eleven, when I felt it would be safest for me to put my plan into action. By that time, Tilly should hopefully be on her way to the airport.

Taking a plate of scrambled eggs with chopped chives and bacon, I found myself a quiet spot, if you could call anywhere quiet with the amount of people milling around. I took in as much as possible of the goings-on amongst my fellow diners, never knowing when something of importance might be said. I paid attention to a group of teenagers, knowing they had an uncanny knack of gravitating towards their own kind with a particular type of finesse.

I recalled, with a mixture of sorrow and amusement, how my own daughters were always making friends within ten minutes whenever we were on holiday. Mealtimes were often overcrowded affairs with plenty of extra guests who just happened to 'drop by'. Thinking of happier times, I took out the photo of Alice and Phoebe, drinking in every detail, as if I didn't know every inch of them already. Just looking at the picture made my heart ache with longing. All three of us depicted wearing our matching Jade seashell necklaces chosen by the girls on our Malaysian family holiday. I fingered my necklace absentmindedly feeling the connection in my mind. Tears prickled at my eyes; I went to put the picture back in my pocket but knocked it to the floor, and I bent to pick it up.

"Can I help?"

I almost fell off my chair, my balance off-kilter from leaning forward.

"I'm sorry," he said, helping me up and picking up the picture, glancing at it before passing it to me. The man seemed vaguely familiar, but I couldn't quite place him.

"Are they your children? They look like you." He was smiling.

I laughed nervously. "No, my nieces," I stammered, flushing. I remembered now; he was one of the other holiday reps at the table the previous day. "I'm sorry, I've forgotten your name. You're a friend of Tilly's, right?"

"Paul, Paul Franks. That's right, though I don't work for the same company as Tilly. We all seem to have the same work schedule now and then however – mind if I join you?" He must have sensed my momentary hesitation, and continued easily, "It sure is packed in here this morning."

"Yes, of course, how rude of me. Where did I expect you to sit, out in reception?" I tried to make light of the matter to cover for my earlier pause. I didn't really want any company at all, but knew I had to try to talk to people; he seemed pleasant enough and if he worked here, he could be valuable.

"Any idea why it's such a madhouse in here this morning?" I couldn't think of anything more interesting to say.

"It's the Disney water park excursion today, at Typhoon Lagoon. It's always a busy one, calls for a large breakfast, but great fun nonetheless." Paul had to shout to make himself heard over the increasing noise.

"Are you on it?" I asked curiously.

"I am, for my sins. If nothing else, it's a great way to dunk a few noisy kids, and it gives the parents a bit of a break. The parks are so well equipped – the security is excellent, so kids can run free while the parents go to the quiet spots and unwind for a while."

"Sounds good to me." I marvelled at the way Paul was so relaxed amidst all the mayhem. Mike would have been complaining of a headache by now, moaning we should have called for room service.

I had to admit, I felt reasonably comfortable with the man sitting opposite me. He couldn't talk much, as children of all ages would recognise him and come over to chat on their way to the breakfast bar.

From what I observed, he never appeared annoyed at the constant barrage of questions; he would just smile, give the answer, ruffle a head and then return to his, now cold, meal.

"I understand you're interested in this line of work?" he asked, obviously remembering my story.

"Yes, I thought I would come and see how it's done." I was about to continue when a small boy of about six came running towards our table, tears streaming down his face.

"I can't find them," he eventually stammered, sobs making up most of the sentence. Paul dropped to his knees, face full of concern.

"Who can't you find, soldier?" His voice was calm and gentle.

"M-my m-mommy a-and daddy,' spluttered the young boy, fresh tears following.

"Don't worry about a thing, we'll go and find them now. I'm sure they must be looking for you, let's go and see." Paul took the little boy's hand in his and turned to me. "Please excuse me, duty calls."

As he said goodbye, I was appalled at myself for finding I considered him attractive, in a rugged sort of way. Together, hand in hand, he and the little boy made their way out of the dining room. I felt a twinge of sadness at his leaving, unsure why. Remembering my plan, I checked my watch; good, it was almost ten thirty, not much longer now. Leaving my table, I paid for breakfast and left the noisy dining area.

The restaurant and gift shop were in the same area as reception and the hotel designated meeting spot, which was designed to look like a road sign. It saved travel reps having to designate individual meeting points, which could easily be forgotten by highly excited holidaymakers. The only drawback to the idea was if there were various excursions taking place at the same time, chaos often ensued; reception and the surrounded areas becoming deluged with people.

I had some time, so went over to the display on one of the walls which held a multiple brochure stand, one of the ones that had the capacity to hold at least fifty or so different brochures, should you care to look. Pretending to look at the numerous Disney, Universal Studios and water theme parks, alongside various other local attractions, I surreptitiously watched tourists gather, meeting their tour guides before boarding their transportation, hoping to catch a glimpse of Alice or Phoebe. Soon, the area was clearing as excursions left for the day. I felt crushed once again for not having seen my children.

The gift shop was small to say the very least. Squeezed between reception and the public telephones, it resembled an oversized store cupboard, packed with the usual array of tack; key rings, postcards, beachwear and flip-flops all on offer. Five minutes of browsing and I was back into the glorious sunshine. I remembered there was a drinks machine on the landing where my room was and decided to pick up a couple of cans.

***

Paul Franks had seen the distraught look on the woman's face; the dropped photo was obviously very precious to her, judging by her reaction when looking at it. The children in the picture looked familiar to him, but he saw so many children's faces every day, he could probably say the same about almost any family photo, he mused. Maybe, if he had time and he remembered, he'd mention something to Tilly when he next saw her. For now, he had the more pressing matter of head counting the non-swimmers for armbands on the Typhoon Lagoon trip.

11.

At eleven exactly, I was back in my room. The air-conditioning unit still wasn't working; turning a few dials and flicking each of the switches on and off, did nothing. With more important things to do, I decided to leave it. My hands were trembling, but to carry out my plan I needed to be calm and collected, so I took a few shaky breaths.

The plan was to call reception pretending to be Tilly. I had to hope I sounded at least a little like her, Tilly was British by birth, and even though she had lived in America for some time, she had no discernible accent.

I was hopeful whoever answered the phone knew Tilly, but not too well; just enough not to over-question or get into too much of a conversation. If that happened, I could probably deal with it, but would rather not have to. I had enough to think about.

I picked up the phone beside my bed and dialled reception. I knew my room number would probably show on the switchboard and just hoped nobody would pay too much attention. I could have made the call from a public phone, but I needed quiet surroundings – somewhere I could think and not be overheard.

"Hello, Drew speaking, how may I help you?"

'Hi Drew, it's Tilly here from Robin's Travel."

"Oh, hi Tilly! How are you today?"

"Good thanks, Drew. I was just wondering if I could check a reservation with you? It's for a party in the name of Weston. They checked in on the 12th and I want to just confirm if they're booked at the hotel for the duration of their stay. I'm sure I had the details but appear to have mislaid them." My hands were shaking uncontrollably. I promised myself that after this was over, I would never attempt anything like this again.

"I'll check for you," Drew replied. There was a lot of efficient tapping of keys; Drew sounded an excellent typist. I caught my reflection in the mirror opposite the bed and saw I was flame-coloured, probably from holding in my nerves. What was taking so long?

"Yep, looks like they're here until 22nd, does that help?"

"Yes, thanks, thanks a million." It was then that I remembered I still didn't have the room number. "Oh, whilst you're on, Drew, did they change their room?" I tried to make the enquiry sound as casual as possible.

"Nope, looks like they're still in 217 – there has been a problem with the water supply on that landing though, so might be worth checking again later, in case some guests have had to be moved," he finished.

"Okay, thanks, bye." I felt I was going to burst and needed to get off the phone.

I sat back, laughing through my tears – I finally had a room number and confirmation that my family was close by. I was closer than ever to knowing for sure where my children were. Never had I been so relieved; my cheeks hurt from grinning. Thanking any deity that happened to be listening, I tried to calm down a little, surprised by my – albeit devious – sense of accomplishment.

Again, I ran through the argument I kept having with myself, the reasons why I couldn't just take the girls as soon as I found them. If I knew for certain where they were, why shouldn't I just barge right in, grab them and get them on the next flight home? I had every right to do to Mike exactly as he had done to me. I had to remind myself of the possible repercussions – if I behaved that way, Alice and Phoebe would be scared witless, possibly even considering that their mother had gone quite mad. That would play right into Mike's hands.

After about an hour of thinking, the euphoria subsided, not as bright or shiny as it was initially. I couldn't bear to lose the girls again, not through my own stupidity. I needed to see them in a state of calm composure, and I had to be patient.

I guessed that all they knew was that they were in America on holiday and, for whatever reason, I wasn't with them. I needed to put my children's feelings before my own. Although Mike had booked a room until the end of the holiday, there was nothing stopping them spending time elsewhere; they may decide to spend a couple of days at the coast, or further south. I tried not to dwell on the question that if they were still at the hotel, why hadn't I bumped into them, or at least had sight of them?

The hotel was arranged in such a way that most activities went on in, or around, the three swimming pools and the main building. Admittedly, I had only been at the hotel for forty-eight hours, but still felt I should have seen them by now.

I decided a good idea would be to familiarise myself with the layout of the three accommodation blocks. My own room, 1020, was on the ground floor of the largest of the blocks. Finding a fire-safety plan, I worked out that Mike's room was on the second floor of the smallest block. Walking around the hotel grounds, I found it and took the stairs, not wanting to take the lift and get stuck having to have conversations with people; I needed to concentrate on the task at hand.

I was surprised to admit to myself, even now, that I was still unsure how I would handle a meeting with Mike. I needed to be in complete control of myself when the time came. Walking towards room 217, I could see the heavy, plastic lined curtains were drawn. I could however see there was no light on in the room from the gap between the curtains. I also noticed there was no incessant hum from the air-conditioning which suggested no one was in the room, nor had been for a while.

Checking there was nobody around, I tried the door – realistically, I knew it would be locked but couldn't stop myself from trying. Defeated, and unsure what to try next, I made my way back through the hotel grounds.

My emotions had swung from elation back to desperation within an hour, exhausting me. Crossing the car park, I spotted Tilly helping her new party of holidaymakers off their coach, guiding them towards the hotel check-in. I was incapable of conversation and knew I wouldn't be able to hide my fragile state from my friend; avoidance was my only option, so I waited until Tilly had gone inside the main building before continuing.

Returning to my room, I felt helpless once more. Laying on the bed and staring at the ceiling, I desperately wanted to talk to someone, mainly to alleviate the wretched loneliness I could feel crawling around inside me. I thought about my daughters, missing everything about them; their touch, their smell, the clutter that accompanied them wherever they went. The smell of burnt toast filling the house every afternoon after school. Their quarrels, and how heated they would get, before laughing again within minutes. Once more, I realised how grateful I was they had each other.

I worked through a million more thoughts until the room became dark. The phone rang once, but I chose to ignore it, knowing it would be Tilly to see if I wanted to go out to eat or for a drink. I didn't want to move; my self-pity was firmly in place and I indulged it gladly.

I woke to the phone ringing again. Fumbling to pick up the receiver, I glanced at my watch seeing it was nine in the evening.

"Hey sleepyhead, what are you up to?" the teasing tone of the familiar, friendly voice was heard.

"Sorry, Tilly, I must've dozed off."

"I tried calling earlier, but you must've been out."

"Oh yes, yes I was. I've been doing a little window shopping," I lied.

"That's the cheapest form of shopping I know," she laughed. "Fancy something to eat? I'm starving."

I thought for a moment; I wasn't hungry at all. I didn't want to be in this hotel, in this room or even in this country. I felt I was treading water and would succumb to drowning in my depression at any moment. What I really wanted to do was wake up and for my life be back to normal again, the nightmare over. Pulling myself together and knowing this wasn't going to happen, I cheerfully replied, "Sounds good to me," hoping I sounded convincing.

"Don't mind if I bring a friend along, do you?"

"No, not at all." In some respects, I did mind – I didn't feel up to socialising at all. I was in America to find my children, and then get them home. Anything else seemed like a waste of precious time, but these people were the only connections I had and I had to stick my story in the hope it led to my children.

"I'm not sure if you met him, his name is Paul." My heart skipped a beat. "I think he was at our table the other morning," Tilly continued.

I certainly remembered the attractive man who had joined me at breakfast, however brief.

"Yes, I remember him," was all I could say. "That would be lovely," I added, aiming for nonchalance.

"Meet you in the lobby in twenty minutes," Tilly said, before hanging up.

* * *

The evening turned out to be a pleasant experience; Tilly was her usual, effervescent self and Paul was a perfect gentleman. His questions to me were never too invasive, yet he obviously wanted to know more about me. I assumed Tilly had filled him in about my 'divorce'; thankfully, I didn't have to remember too many details which meant I wasn't in much danger of tripping myself up.

The food was simple, and although my appetite had waned considerably, stress taking its place, what I ate was delicious. I returned that night to my room in a much better frame of mind. Still uncertain as to what to do next, I reasoned decisions didn't have to be made hastily – there were still a few days to go before the end of both my family's holiday and my own. I slept a little better that night, trying to reason that the day had some positive aspects – I just had to be patient with my planning.

My fourth day in America brought about two major decisions. The first, and least important, was to get the air conditioning fixed in my room. The second was my next move regarding Mike. I would start with observing the room he and the girls were staying in, keeping an eye out for any comings and goings – I still needed confirmation that my family was actually staying in the room. I needed to see them with my own eyes. Once I knew that, I would continue watching – I knew the safest solution would be to wait until nearer the departure date to make my move, giving Mike no time to come up with any new plans, or disappear.

My intent was to get Alice and Phoebe out of the country and back to England with the minimum amount of fuss. I figured the best way to do this would be by acting as if I had joined them all for the end of the holiday; then I would leave with my children. Of course, how well my plan would work depended on what story Mike had told the twins., but how he got himself out of whatever pack of lies he had told was his own problem. Once home, my task would be to try and make life as normal as possible for the three of us.

I decided that once I had confirmed the whereabouts of my children, and made sure they were safe, I would keep a low profile until I was ready to make my appearance. I questioned whether I should stay locked in my room until the time was right. Even if Mike had taken Alice and Phoebe elsewhere for part of their holiday, I was fairly confident that he would return a day or so before they were due to return home, given the hotel reservations, the close proximity to the airport and the major attractions. This, again, was dependent on Mike's intention to return to England, of which there was no guarantee. I decided not to dwell too much on that possibility.

With my sparse wardrobe dwindling rapidly, a small amount of shopping was becoming a necessity, rather than a once pleasurable act. Showering, changing into my final set of clean clothes and putting in a quick call to reception to get someone to fix the air-conditioning, I left my room; the heat was stifling.

Fortunately, the hotel was situated on one side of International Drive; the other, with a pedestrian crossing of mammoth proportions, led to a recently built shopping complex. I felt I now had a need for a disguise of some sort, allowing me to move around without being noticed.

With one pair of dark, oversized sunglasses, my hair tied back in a ponytail, and a baseball cap later, I felt confident enough to walk around with the droves of tourists. Ironically, at one point I would have loved for my children, or even Mike for that matter, to have recognised me but this was no longer the case.

If there was one thing Orlando could offer, it was the ability to blend into the crowds effortlessly and within half an hour, I began to relax a little. The variety of shops available in such a relatively small space astounded me. The complex was set out over two floors, with shops selling authentic Chinese artifacts, furniture and even carpets, alongside the likes of GAP, Sunglass Hut, Calvin Klein and Elizabeth Arden. One corner portion of the ground floor was given up to FAO Schwartz Toy Shop, and was built in brightly coloured concrete, complete with a concrete rag doll that stood at least ten feet high, looking for all the world like it was holding up the front of the shop. An even bigger concrete teddy bear and spinning top did the same feat for the other sides of the store.

After almost two hours of browsing, I felt the waves of panic crash over me again; even though I had made the decision to hold back on making an appearance, I was still searching every face I saw for the familiar smiles of my children. As my mood began to darken, I saw a Sizzler restaurant and felt I needed to sit down. It was on the same side of the Drive as the hotel, and I hoped I would, at the very least, feel closer to where my daughters might be. Positioning myself at a table that offered a partial view of the accommodation block which housed room 217, I ordered the first thing I saw on the menu, surveillance easy amidst the busy lunch-time crowd. Having a self-service salad bar meant I was able to walk all around the restaurant without drawing any attention, and keep an eye on both the hotel entrance and exit driveways.

I sat for what seemed like a lifetime, staring at the door of 217, pushing the food around my plate, having given up on eating after only a couple of forkfuls. I knew I needed to keep strong for my children, I was no good to them otherwise – I shouldn't be allowing negativity to take over my thoughts. There still had been no sign of any movement in the room. The curtains, as far as I could see, remained drawn. I was becoming consumed by frustration at not having seen something; anything would have been better than this.

Another few minutes passed before I paid my bill, leaving a generous tip, and headed back to the hotel. I saw Tilly as I emerged from the restaurant and made my way over to her, dodging the constant flow of tour-operated charter coaches winding their way through the hotel's one way system.

Tilly didn't recognise me, almost walking straight past me; I was delighted my disguise was so effective.

"Going to ignore me?" I asked playfully.

"Wow, Julia, you going undercover?" she laughed.

"No, just thought I'd blend in a little, you know, when in Rome and all that."

"I'll say, you look positively native," grinned Tilly. "Fancy a coffee?"

I felt I couldn't eat or drink another thing, but the coffee shop had a covered outdoor area which offered a great view of the entrance and exit to the hotel, an excellent spot to continue my surveillance.

"Love to," I replied.

Falling into step with my friend, Tilly filled me in with the details of the day's events. Children getting lost, pensioners having too much sun, and overly amorous twenty-something's trying their luck seemed to be the general run of things. I thanked Tilly again for the previous evening and asked her to pass on my thanks to Paul.

"I think he's very interested in you," Tilly ventured cautiously.

"He was a nice man, but I'm not interested in getting involved with anybody right now." It was a knee jerk reply; I didn't want to offend my friend, but I wasn't totally convinced I wasn't saying it as much to myself, as to reply to my friend's statement.

"I can understand that, but don't be surprised if he just happens to turn up at the same places you happen to be," Tilly teased. I allowed myself to laugh along, relaxing a little.

"Well, it's a free country," I added flippantly. We sat and drank coffee, during which I discreetly kept an eye on the entry and exit barriers. Although I couldn't see the room from where I was sitting, I felt just as much importance should be placed on the whole hotel – if the twins had gone out with their father, they'd have to return at some point.

12.

Letting myself into my room and turning on the light, there was a scribbled note from maintenance on the table beside the window, saying they hadn't been able to fix the air-conditioning unit. It suggested a discount on my room rate, or a change of room, if preferred. My mind raced; if I could get a room close to Mike's, I would be in a better position to observe.

Immediately, I rang reception and explained the contents of the note. I tried my luck, asking if I could get another room, in the two hundreds perhaps. I thought it would seem a little suspicious if I were more specific. The desk clerk came back with an offer of room 212. Remembering the hotel plan, this room was on the other side of the block to Mike's. Claiming that the noise of the interstate may be too much, I asked if there was anything on the other side available.

This time the clerk came back with room 221, which was perfect, being next door but one to Mike's. All I needed was for the occupants of room 219 to be nice and quiet, and for Alice and Phoebe to make enough noise, and I'd know if they were around. Just thinking of my children for more than a minute brought tears to my eyes and I ached to hold them in my arms.

Holding back my emotions as best I could, I focused on the task at hand. Arrangements were made and I would move rooms the following morning.

I woke early to prepare for my short, yet significant, move. I gave the small bathroom a quick clean and made the beds – how I had managed to disrupt both queen sized beds, I couldn't recollect – but they were both restored to their former neatness.

By eight that morning, I was re-packed, not that I'd really unpacked properly anyway. Double-checking all the drawers were empty on my way out, I was safely ensconced in my new room ten minutes later. The hotel was built so that each landing had access at both ends via stairs, with a lift in the middle. I used the stairs furthest from my room, enabling me to get to my door without having to walk past room 217.

I didn't want to get spotted yet, though I felt fairly confident that Mike wouldn't recognise me anyway, not with my new disguise in place. I couldn't, however, say the same for my daughters. I had a feeling they would know me regardless.

The interior of the new room was identical to the previous one, although the bedspread – which I assumed were standard issue to all hotels – was a slightly different floral pattern. The air-conditioning was drumming away to itself quite nicely, and I found the noise inexplicably comforting.

Straining my ears, I tried desperately to heighten my senses, hoping to tune into something that would help identify my children, be it a laugh, cough or the sound of a voice.

There was nothing besides the droning. Maybe it was too early to be expecting to hear anything other than air-conditioning units battling against the humidity of Florida, or the occasional sounding of a horn in the distance. It was also possible that the usual activities of early morning had already taken place.

I swore the not knowing would kill me at this rate. The rest of the day, I decided, would be devoted once again to surveillance; mainly because I couldn't come up with anything else that would prove more productive. My intuition told me that Mike's room was unoccupied, as was my neighbour's. As I walked along the landing, I noticed all the rooms seemed to be quiet – in fact, mine was the only one that looked occupied. I then thought I was allowing my mind to run away with me and upon checking my watch, I saw it was nine thirty, time for breakfast.

On my way through the main building, I checked out what laundry facilities the hotel offered, discovering that all I needed to do was collect a pink bag and fill it with the clothes I wanted cleaning, before leaving the bag outside my room.

Finding my usual spot in the dining room, I bade good morning to the waiter. Collecting my breakfast of eggs with chives and bacon, I made myself comfortable and began people watching. Over the last few days, I'd discovered I had quite a talent for observing details; they gave away a lot about a person.

I gleaned from overheard conversations from the family sitting in front of me that they were on a once in a lifetime holiday. They took time to make the most out of every moment, and the children, of whom there were two, were very polite and extremely well behaved. It appeared they weren't necessarily accustomed to having everything they wanted and almost had to be persuaded by their parents to enjoy all that was on offer. I had fought back an onset of tears just watching them.

It was through their parent's lead, after long, protracted breakfasts, that they began to relax and enjoy trying the different dishes that were on offer, though never to excess. I often heard comments from the parents such as 'we've waited a long time for this, so let's enjoy ourselves' – even they seemed to have difficulty in adjusting to the abundance of offerings thrust at them.

Sometimes, I allowed myself a twinge of optimism, telling myself that I would get my daughters back. It would soon subside when I began to consider the enormity of the task and considered just what the odds were of finding anybody in this place. Often, I would have to look away from the family, having been reminded of my own loss. I was, however, unable to make myself change tables, the torture almost like a drug, needed, but only just endured.

From the overheard snippets of conversation, I would smile at their renditions of visits to Disney, dinner at King Henry's Feast, Church Street Station and the Hard Rock Café. The children, boys aged about eight and six, would have a competition every morning, trying to outdo each other with what they had done the previous day. They had, of course, done exactly the same thing, but it was a contest of who could claim the most satisfaction and entertainment.

I realised I was envious of this ordinary family, who were enjoying a much-loved and long awaited holiday. They didn't wear designer clothes, nor sport the latest accessories. They had probably saved for quite some time for this trip and were loving every minute of it. The envy consumed me.

Self-pity, once again, dug its claws deep into my heart. What had I done to deserve this? Thoroughly depressed, I left my untouched breakfast and decided to go for a walk. Heading out of reception and into the blazing sun, I found myself going towards the shopping complex I had visited the previous day. I wasn't moving in any particular direction; I was drifting, like a boat lost at sea.

Grateful for the hordes of people milling about, I mused that it seemed as though shopping was almost a twenty-four hour activity in Orlando; certainly it was here on International Drive, anyway. Nobody appeared to notice the tears of sorrow etching their way down my face as I made my way in and out of almost every store, oblivious to their contents. I had never felt so alone.

I watched the masses of people around me, all of them weaving one way, then the next, no one sure who the leader was but all following the person in front as if they held the key to happiness, saw the best things, spotted the greatest bargain. I smiled as I saw the clutches of teenagers hanging around the shops and scattered seating areas; the boys were desperately trying to impress with clever remarks and cool charm, the girls giggling too much, switching between flirting and appearing aloof.

I thought about Phoebe and Alice, what they might be up to, and what they had seen and done – all without their mother. I was torturing myself; they were probably having a great time. Wearily, I began walking in the direction of the hotel, which I now viewed as my self-imposed prison.

***

Lilly had had a hard day. There had been two incidents on the trip, both unnerving. The first, an elderly gentleman had suffered what appeared to be a mild heart attack, his poor wife becoming hysterical and having to receive medical assistance alongside her husband. Fortunately, the man had survived and was now comfortable in one of Orlando's many hospitals, his wife by his side.

The second was a strange occurrence that Tilly had replayed in her head at least a dozen times already. The trip had been to Universal Studios, a favourite of Tilly's; she never tired of the constantly evolving park. The group had included quite a few teenagers, all of whom had been well behaved and helpful in distracting the younger children's attention when the old man had taken ill. Tilly had arranged for medical assistance and was waiting for the ambulance to arrive to take the elderly couple to the hospital, when a couple of teenage girls had asked if she needed any help.

Initially, she couldn't quite put her finger on why they seemed so familiar. In a flash, she saw they were smaller, younger carbon copies of her friend, Julia. Their eyes were slightly different, but everything else was identical. They were obviously twins; it was almost impossible to tell them apart. She recalled Paul mentioning something about a photo that he had seen Julia looking at of two girls and, from the description he gave, these had to be the same girls, surely.

She had a compelling need to know more about them. Thanking them for their offer and explaining the casualties would soon be on their way to the hospital, she invited them for coffee and doughnuts at the diner. The girls waited with Tilly until the ambulance arrived and the elderly couple were safely on their way, accompanied by another travel rep, before slowly walking together to the circular, sixties-style diner, chatting easily.

Tilly had grown immune to the charms of the establishment's collection of film and music memorabilia, all from another era, but her companions were bowled over, enamoured with the waitresses zipping about masterfully on roller skates, avoiding customers and providing entertainment and refreshments at the same time.

They were awestruck with the photographs signed by Hollywood greats, which included the likes of Clark Gable, Meryl Streep, The Beatles, The Rolling Stones, and so many more. They changed their orders three times before deciding on cappuccinos and large, chocolate covered doughnuts. Though a little unadventurous, cappuccinos were certainly the coolest drink to order and be seen drinking, they informed her.

Tilly smiled at both girls, they were so animated and very polite. She hadn't seen the girls before on any of the other day trips and asked them if they had been staying at the Quality Inn Plaza long. They said that they were on holiday with their father, and that they had a room at the hotel but had been staying at other places too. They had begged their father to let them go on a trip by themselves. Eventually relenting, he allowed it on the condition that it was a trip organised by the hotel, and so they had booked themselves on the Universal Studios excursion. They pointed out that they were, after all, not children anymore, and they wanted to be treated like adults.

Indeed, the two were mature in their conduct, though there was still an air of childishness about them, almost as if they had lived slightly sheltered lives. Tilly thought perhaps they enjoyed the privilege of private education.

She asked them about the places that they had visited so far and they told her that they had been to the Florida Keys and had loved Key West; they even had their photograph taken with the Ernest Hemingway lookalike outside Sloppy Joes.

Tilly could hold back no longer and asked, "Is your mother joining you for your holiday?"

The girls fell silent. It was Phoebe, the more outspoken of the two, who answered.

"She isn't well at the moment, so she didn't come on holiday with us." The young girl sounded close to tears, and Tilly felt bad for asking.

"Oh, I'm sorry to hear that, I hope she gets better soon," Tilly offered.

"We had no idea she was ill, until Daddy told us. We had to keep the holiday a secret because Daddy said Mummy needed to have some special treatment, and if she found out about the holiday, she would want to come along and delay her treatment. Daddy said it was very important that she had the treatment as soon as possible, to make sure she got well again."

"I bet it must have been hard for the two of you to have to try and keep it a secret."

"Oh, it was awful," said Phoebe. "We nearly gave the game away once or twice. I don't like keeping secrets from Mummy," added Alice nervously fingering the necklace she wore. Tilly was sure she had seen the distinctive necklace before, she noticed then that both girls were wearing identical Jade seashell necklaces.

At that point, another teenager approached the table and he obviously wanted to talk to the twins. He had a shock of red hair that was masterfully gelled into a sea of tiny, shiny spikes. For all his bravado, he wasn't too sure of himself and his face reddened with lightning speed as he politely interrupted, asking if the twins might like to join his group of friends for some of the rides.

They both turned to Tilly, as if she was now their guardian and, she guessed, also out of politeness. She explained she had quite a few things to be getting on with and thought it would be a lovely idea for them to join their friends. The girls, pleased with the show of enthusiasm from an adult for fun, rapidly slurped the final dregs of the cappuccinos and followed the red-haired boy.

The encounter had bothered Tilly greatly, a small voice in her head told her there was definitely a link between the two girls and her friend. She had no proof as to what it was, and nothing to substantiate her feelings, other than their striking resemblance to Julia, and even that could be a matter of opinion. There was something else, she was sure but couldn't place her finger on what it was that made her feel so sure of the connection. She had heard of people having doubles, but even that wasn't applicable as these were two young girls. It also wasn't just a case of physical attributes, but also of mannerisms, something which can't be put down to coincidence.; seeing someone hold a cup or brush their hair back whilst talking the same way, is something that was picked up by learning, by being around someone for long periods of time, influenced.

Tilly thought back to her initial meeting with Julia, and their subsequent outings. Julia had never once mentioned children, in fact, she seemed to recall that she had specifically said she *didn't* have any. Paul had said that Julia, when questioned, claimed the children in the photo were her nieces, and Tilly was sure she had mentioned something about a family connection in the area.

She pushed her thoughts to the back of her mind and busied herself with the rest of the party, making sure everybody was having a good time, enjoying all that Universal had to offer.

When shepherding everybody back onto the coach at the end of the afternoon, she had to admit she was grateful her day was coming to an end. She paid special attention to the large group of teenagers that Phoebe and Alice had joined, making sure they were safely accounted for, telling herself it was part of normal procedure and not because, for some reason, she felt a responsibility to the two girls she had only recently met.

The drive back to the hotel was only a short distance, but they had hit the five o'clock traffic, so it was sluggish. She half turned in her seat and watched the youngsters talking animatedly to each other, occasionally cracking the odd joke, and generally having fun. Tilly noticed the twins were able to hold a conversation with others as one person; one would fill in odd words, never talking over each other, merely operating as one unit. She had never seen anything like it. None of the rest of the group seemed to notice, or care.

The more Tilly watched them both, the more she was convinced. She needed to find Julia and talk to her. There was no reason to doubt her friend's story, but she had a feeling that there was much more to it than she had been told. Before long, the coach drew to a halt, air brakes squealing with released pressure. The crowd took some time to get their belongings and alight from the vehicle, still excited from their day's outing. Tilly knew she wouldn't be able to talk to Julia that evening; she would have to go to the hospital to check on the progress of the elderly couple and to relieve her colleague, who had accompanied the couple to the hospital earlier.

A phone call to the hospital revealed that the elderly man was doing very well, but the couple had decided they wanted to return to England, when the doctors gave the okay. Tilly said that she understood their wishes and would organise the necessary details and would see them both a little later.

By the time Tilly had sent the necessary paperwork through to the head office in London and filed her incident report, it was late evening. Filling a small bag with a few items she thought the couple may find useful and a quick change of clothes for herself, she collected the car and made her way downtown towards the hospital. The gentle country music she had on the radio soothed her mind, which for the time being, was only occupied with manoeuvres needed to keep one step ahead of the locals driving their large Buicks and Continentals against the now driving rain, which had begun as gentle drizzle hours earlier.

After fifteen minutes, she was able to find a space in the parking lot of the modern hospital. She found the elderly couple, comfortable in a private room and very pleased to see her. She had a quick and informal chat with her colleague who had accompanied the couple, checked their details matched the day's events and made sure her report read correctly. Once this was done, she dismissed her colleague and gave her the next day off, knowing that it would be much appreciated.

The form for 'alien admittance', the name given to a holidaymaker or non-resident of the United States admitted to a hospital, was formidable and had to be precise. The questions often seemed almost ridiculous but were viewed as highly important to the hospital and insurance companies alike. Tilly stayed at the hospital until after midnight, ensuring all was well for the couple and helping them feel as comfortable as possible until they would be allowed to begin their long journey back home.

13.

I had got as far as the main straight of International Drive, and found my feet taking me left, back up the Drive, passing the enormous array of garish shops and hotels situated on either side. One of the hotels was built in the style of a castle, though not the dull brown or grey variety; this one was completely pink with a pale blue roof and turrets, reached only via a mock drawbridge. There were mini-golf courses set out amongst man-made pirate's coves and shipwrecks. The unusual stood out all the more against the backdrop of more established hotels and motels, most with a similar format of large concrete blocks. In between the hotels, were the standard buffet-style restaurants, all offering a huge mixture of steak, fish, salad and barbeque; there were even some oriental eateries that offered an 'all you can eat' experience at certain times of the day.

Factory outlets and dollar shops sat side by side with Calvin Klein, Donna Karan and more designers, than I had ever seen in such a small area. The tacky and the luxurious made up the crazy patchwork of International Drive. It was amazing how everyday life was also apparent amongst the wonderland that made this place what it was; there were buses collecting office workers and school children, commuters in their air-conditioned cars, listening to the million and one radio stations available. The cars made mini rivulets on the toasting tarmac, as their air-conditioning systems battled against the constant humidity, attempting desperately to create a comfortable environment.

Coming to a set of traffic lights which divided International Drive in half, I continued northwards, flanked on either side by a sea of hotels, shops and restaurants. To the east, the road looked like it headed to downtown Orlando, the business district. To the west was an interstate intersection, the sign stated 'Interstate 4' and headed towards Tampa. Running parallel with the Drive, it ran across the back of the hotels, on the same side as the Quality Inn Plaza.

I turned back on myself and headed in the direction I had come, the dark cloud of depression I had tried to keep at bay becoming oppressive once more. The heat by now was furious, and most people were diving into shops just to cool down. Being alone seemed to make time slow down to an unbearable level; it also heightened my sense of loss and the physical ache that never seemed to leave these days.

There were times when the enormity of my situation would make me question why I was in one of the largest countries in the world, trying to find three people. It wasn't only one of the largest countries, but the area in which I was looking was so heavily populated, by both the people that live here and the millions that visited all year round. What hope did I really have of finding my family?

There was still no solid proof that Mike and the girls were even at the hotel, the town or even still in the country. I was trying to work on a mixture of guesswork and assumption – not the most exacting science. When I reached the depths of despair, there would then begin the positive thinking, the pep talk, the self-convincing that eventually allowed me to think that my patience would pay off and be rewarded. It didn't make what seemed like an eternity any easier to bear, but it was necessary to stave off the ever threatening dark cloud.

My mind drifted to my old friend Marcia, wondering what she would be doing. Probably playing the suffering widow to perfection, allowing her clique of friends to offer their insincere condolences. Marcia's family had too much money and influence to be shunned for their daughter's loss and the drama surrounding it. In such circles, scandals are dealt with in two ways; those families that have great and long-standing social bearing will be surrounded by a profusion of sympathy, with offers of yachts, apartments or villas as places to recuperate from such a trauma. If you were of the less historic and influential standing – the newly wealthy – you would be shut out almost instantly.

People, as a rule, have two types of friends: real friends, who stand by regardless of a situation, and fair-weather friends, who are only friends when it's advantageous for them to be such. I had come to realize I had become a member of society predominantly made up of the latter type. Mike and Alex's success was down to hard work, determination and diligence – they had no history, none of any worth anyway, having risen from nothing. Only when successful had they been admitted to the privileged sect. Marcia had always been there; I couldn't comprehend now, how we had ever been so close.

Tilly then came into my thoughts, as if offering a subconscious comparison. The deceit I felt at using Tilly's friendship was unbelievable, and I wondered if I had joined the ranks of those who only befriended a person for their own gain. I genuinely felt such great warmth towards her and knew she deserved better. I reminded myself however, that nothing must come between me and getting my children back.

Not having realised it, I had reached the hotel. I spent a restless evening wandering the grounds, keeping an eye on Mike's room as best I could, whilst drinking too much coffee. The sun had disappeared, leaving a clear sky with stars twinkling brightly; feeling chilly, I decided to go to bed.

After letting myself into the room, I knew nothing had changed at room 217. The curtains were in the same, drawn position, no lights were burning, the air-conditioning system still wasn't on and there wasn't even any condensation on the windows to suggest occupancy; the signs were not looking good. All was quiet, the barely audible sound of the nearby Interstate only becoming apparent when someone using it felt the need to beep their horn.

The next morning took the same routine. The heat was so oppressive that, within five minutes of being without air conditioning, I felt sticky, miserable and irritable. Already on my third cup of coffee at the hotel's café, I stared blankly towards the horizon, unaware of anybody else.

"Mind if I sit down for a while?"

Turning to see Tilly, I smiled. "Of course not." I was pleased to see my friend and my spirits lifted a little. "I've been doing a little more job research." I didn't sound convincing, and I knew it.

"Julia, I consider you a friend and as such, I want you to know that you can trust me." This sounded ominous. I looked at my friend opposite, trying to read the look in her eyes. Had somebody said something? Had I been spotted skulking around the hotel trying to keep an eye on room 217 and been reported as being suspicious? I felt ashamed.

"Why do you say that?" I tried to smile and lighten the conversation but failed miserably. For some reason, I was close to tears. She took my hand and looked into my eyes.

"'I would like you to tell me the real reason why you're here in America, but before you do, I need you to know that the reason I ask is so that I can help, or at least, I think I can help." Tilly sounded sincere, and took a deep breath before continuing, "If you can tell me the truth now, it will go no further and I'm sure I can help you, I really want to."

I looked Tilly in the eye and knew I could trust her. Voice shaking, I decided to go for broke.

"A few days ago, though it now seems like a lifetime ago, my world fell apart. It started with a disconnected mobile phone and continued with finding out my home had been sold out from under my nose. My husband's business had been shut down by the authorities and he's under investigation for embezzlement. His business partner committed suicide and his wife, my best friend at the time, disappeared. To round things off, my husband has now taken our children on an alleged holiday. All of this occurred in approximately twenty-four hours." My voice was faltering as I relived the horror of my situation. Fresh tears fell silently, unchecked, and despair flooded my body once more; I felt I might never survive this ordeal.

"God, Julia, and you've been carrying this baggage around with you all this time?" Tilly questioned, eyes wide.

"What else could I do, who else could I turn to? The police are only interested in missing people when they're actually missing. I know where my children are, or at least I have a very good idea. Their father, for all his sins, wouldn't hurt them. Christ, their headmistress even has a letter requesting permission to remove them from school, to take them on this supposed vacation." I was wiping the tears from my face.

"Your children are twin girls, right?"

I froze. "How did you know that?" I tried desperately to run through any conversations where I may have said something, may have given away the fact that I even had children, but I knew I hadn't said a word.

"I know because I've seen them, and by the way, they're a real credit to you." Tilly smiled, as if trying to reassure me.

I was powerless to stem the sobs that escaped from deep within me.

"It's okay, it's okay, they're fine, really, I promise." Tilly's eyes filled with tears.

"When did you see them? How did you know that they were my daughters? Was Mike with them? Oh god, are they really okay?" I fired the questions rapidly, not daring to believe my search was over.

"They were absolutely fine, I promise. I saw them yesterday. I didn't know for sure that they were your children, but, Julia, I swear I have never met or seen children that have such a striking resemblance to their parent, namely you. They are the spitting image of you. Seeing you now, there is one more thing that means there is no mistaking they are your children...you're are all three wearing the same necklaces."

I felt for my necklace, it was true we wore the necklaces all the time, never taking them off since the family holiday.

"No one was with them – they apparently had nagged their father to let them do something on their own. He relented and they were allowed to go on one of the hotel's trips to Universal Studios, which I just so happened to be taking," Tilly finished triumphantly, wiping away her own tears.

"I have to tell you, there is someone else looking out for you – Paul. He mentioned something to me about a family photo you had, and your distress when looking at it. Paul's remark, the girls' resemblance to you and then the matching necklaces... there is only so much coincidence can account for."

I didn't know what to think or say regarding Tilly's remark about Paul looking out for me, so I let it hang, unanswered.

"Did they say anything to you?" I wanted to hear every single detail, feeling suddenly close to my children just hearing of them.

Tilly continued, "I had somewhat of an eventful day yesterday, an elderly man had a heart attack and your daughters asked if there was anything they could do to help. The gentleman and his wife were taken to hospital and, as way of a thank you, I offered to buy the girls a coffee at the diner. They told me they were on holiday with their father, as I said." There was a moment of hesitation, before she ploughed forward.

"They also told me the reason why their mum wasn't with them was because she was ill and had to stay at home for treatment."

"Ill?" I parroted back at her, unable to believe what I had just heard.

"Yes, they said that they had been told by their father not to mention the holiday to their mum as she needed some treatment urgently, and if she found out they were going on holiday, she wouldn't have it, and would instead come on holiday and not get better." These words tumbled out in a rush, as if she thought she had to get through it quickly.

I stirred my coffee, unable to believe what I had just heard, turning every detail over in my mind. Mike had known the girls would do anything he said – how could he use his own daughters like this? Like pawns in his own sick game.

A silence fell between us, both caught up in the web of deceit that had been created. I was unable to believe I knew so little about the man who was my husband; never would I have thought he was capable of any of the actions, lies or deceptions he had carried out with such conviction. He was a stranger to me.

We looked out over the gardens surrounding the café; the shimmering heat was rising on the horizon, the temperature increasing by the minute. Regardless, I felt chilled. Considering what Tilly already knew, I knew I had to tell the rest of the story, beginning with my departure from England and how I managed to get myself to America and finishing with how, through deceit of my own, I had managed to find out where Mike had taken Alice and Phoebe.

I admitted, somewhat ashamedly, how I had posed as Tilly to confirm Mike's stay at the hotel and his room number. Surprisingly, Tilly found this highly amusing, even congratulating me on being so resourceful. I told her of my daily surveillance of room 217, relaying how I hadn't seen any activity at the room whatsoever and was getting worried. All things now said, I fell silent.

14.

Tilly sat quietly for a moment, absorbing, I assume, all she had been told. I hoped for forgiveness but would understand if she felt too betrayed by my behaviour for our friendship to continue. Regardless, I felt as though a huge weight had been lifted from my shoulders. Finally, I had talked to somebody who had listened. After what seemed like an eternity, Tilly spoke.

"I think what you need is a little help."

I almost missed the words, spoken quietly and with determination.

"Oh, Tilly, I wouldn't dream of asking you to put yourself, or your job, in jeopardy."

"You didn't ask me to," she retorted, smiling.

"Why would you want to help?" Even now, ashamedly, I was suspicious, unable to believe that anyone would want to get involved in my sordid dilemma.

"I'm your friend. Friends help each other out." Tilly smiled simply. "Now, if you say you can't make an appearance until nearer the end of the holiday, we need to try and keep an eye on the goings-on of your husband and your daughters, so they don't disappear. We also need to keep you as occupied as much as possible, so that you don't drive yourself any further insane." I smiled at my friend's description of me, she had a point.

"You say you haven't seen any activity at all in room 217?"

"That's right. I haven't even seen any sign of them around the hotel," I added miserably. I realised what a miracle it was that Tilly had spotted my girls the previous day, especially in the sea of what must have been hundreds of kids.

"Right then, what I'll do is check to see who is on reception now. If it's who I think it is, I can get a key and we can go and check out the room. If there's no evidence that your family is staying there, I can contact some of my colleagues working at some of the other hotels on the Drive and see if they're staying at any of those."

"I really am grateful to you, Tilly, and please, please accept my apologies for deceiving you. I should have known better." Worried, I asked, "Are you really sure you won't get yourself into trouble?"

"Honey, I promise you, this is nothing compared to some of the things I have had to do in the past. I'm happy to help."

***

Tilly left her companion whilst she went to reception. As she suspected, Romano was working the front desk and he had a soft spot for Tilly; he'd been trying to get her to go on a date with him for weeks. She smiled sweetly as she approached the desk.

"'Hello, Romano."

"Hi, Tilly," he replied in his strong Italian accent. "How may I help you today?"

"If you wouldn't mind, could you check something out for me, please?"

"Of course." A beautiful white smile beamed back at her.

"I'd like to know the name of the guest staying in room 217."

"Let's see now." He tapped furiously at the computer. "Room 217 has a Mr and Mrs Johnson booked, but not until tomorrow. At present, the room is unoccupied." Triumphant with his information, he flashed Tilly another grin.

"I see." Tilly deliberately sounded confused. "Could you possibly tell me what room a Mr Weston is staying in? I've found a set of car keys outside the door of room 217 and assumed they belonged to the occupant – glad I thought to check first." Romano was listening to her whilst merrily tapping away once again at his keyboard.

"There is a Mr Weston in room 271, same block but different landing." Romano looked a little puzzled.

"Silly me, I meant 271," she giggled. A little over the top she thought to herself, but Romano could have been told there were pigs flying outside in the car park and he might just have believed her. As it was, the story she was giving made zero sense either way but she was right in thinking he was too happy to be chatting to her to notice the flaws. "I don't suppose you could give me the spare keys for 271? I can then leave the lost keys on the table for the owner's return."

Romano hesitated for a moment, before relenting. "Okay, Tilly, but you have to return the key before my shift ends. You know I have to have everything in order before I can sign off."

"Of course, Romano, I'll have them back to you in a flash." Tilly beamed at the Italian.

Romano handed Tilly the spare key and she allowed her hand to rest on his a fraction too long – she would pay for that later, but it was all for a good cause, and he wasn't hard on the eyes either.

Tilly sashayed her way through the somewhat busy coffee shop, knowing her Italian admirer's eyes were watching her every move, and returned to the table where Julia sat. She knew she was still being watched, so made polite conversation with a family at the next table. When she was sure she was no longer under observation, she whispered 'follow me' into Julia's ear – she was actually quite enjoying herself, getting quite caught up in the cloak and dagger routine.

***

Making our way to the accommodation block which housed room 271, I kept eye on what was happening around us, not wanting to be seen looking suspicious and thinking how awful it would be to be caught out at this late stage. I carefully followed Tilly through the gardens and along the pathways, trying desperately to look as casual as possible.

Tilly stopped at a suitable place where there was nobody around and certainly not within earshot.

"Your family is in room 271, not 217. I don't know who gave you the room number, but they either got it wrong or you must have misheard." Tilly said. "Anyway, I got the spare key for 271. I'm going to go up there and knock on the door. If somebody answers, I can say I'm there to invite the twins to join me on another hotel excursion. I'm sure they'll jump at the chance, they seemed to have had such a good time on the last one, and it would be no problem for me to squeeze them on one anyway. If there's nobody in the room, I'll give a signal and you can have a quick look to make sure it's the right room. I'll leave a note if there's no one there, inviting the girls out." I was impressed at Tilly's ingenuity. I could have kissed her, feeling like there was someone on my side, at last.

"Let's do it." I was buzzing now, adrenaline pumping through my body and I couldn't wait any longer.

***

Tilly made her way purposefully up the flights of concrete stairs, her speech ready. Pausing for a moment at the door, she smoothed down the blue skirt of her uniform, straightened her jacket, took a deep breath and smiled brightly. She knocked three times loudly, in part, in case the television was on, but also because she'd realised her hands were shaking and wasn't sure she could stand the suspense if she had to knock again to get herself heard.

Suddenly, the door sprung open.

"Yeeez, what do you want?" the chambermaid bellowed loudly, clearly annoyed at being disturbed during her work.

Tilly was thrown a little.

"I'm sorry, I was looking for the occupants, I have something of theirs to return," she stammered.

"Gone out they 'ave, for de 'ole day, lovely family, be back tonight," the chambermaid once again barked in an undetermined accent, folding her well-padded arms across a vast bosom, as if to signify the end of the conversation.

"I see, okay, well perhaps I'll call back later then." Tilly was lost for anything further to say and turned on her heel, heading back down the stairs.

***

She walked straight passed me and I quickly followed her. We didn't speak until we got to the café.

"Well, that gave me a shock I can tell you," Tilly laughed.

"Were they in?" I asked, still not knowing what had happened, being out of earshot.

"They weren't, but the maid was, and she was not happy at being interrupted, let me tell you."

"God, the waiting is unbearable. How long do they take on each room, do you know?" I was impatient now, so close to finally getting some real answers.

"No more than about twenty minutes usually. We'll give it half an hour and can try again." Tilly sounded out of breath; she had obviously been caught off guard.

We sat for what seemed like an age, looking out at the people coming and going, neither saying much as the tension became almost too much to bear. I couldn't take my eyes of the block where Mike's room was, drawn to it.

Eventually, the minutes passed. We retraced our steps silently, neither daring to say anything. As we got closer, Tilly passed the key to me and I went in front. I could hear my own breathing coming out in loud gasps and my heartbeat sounded so loud that I was sure all could hear it, half-expecting security to appear any moment.

I knocked loudly, then waited for what seemed like an eternity. I prayed the maid had gone, not knowing what I would have said had I encountered her. I could wait no longer; my hands shook as I slid the key into the barrel and turned the handle. There was almost no resistance and the door sprang gently open, flooding light into the dark room.

I hesitated for a moment before entering the room, feeling for the light switch in the gloom. As soon as the lights came on, I knew this was where my daughters were staying. Stifling a sob, I absorbed my surroundings; it was just like home. Phoebe and Alice had dropped various items of clothing on their way to and from the bathroom and it was obvious that the girls were sharing one of the beds, sleeping top-to-toe. The maid must have realised this, as pyjamas were neatly folded at each end of the bed.

Alice's pink dressing gown was dangling from underneath one pillow, while Phoebe's hair accessories were strewn over her pillow. Touching my daughters' possessions, I felt their presence. My body was consumed by the dull ache of longing, the desire to feel my children in my arms, smell their hair; it was just too much to bear. I cried into the soft fabric of their night clothes. Never had I wanted something so bad as to have my babies with me once again and I allowed myself to grieve for a few moments. The bed nearest the window was Mike's, and it was just as neat as the rest of the room; clearly, the maid had been busy.

From the items I could see, there was no evidence of anyone else occupying the room other than my family. I was relieved for the sake of my daughters; they would have enough to deal with. I had half-expected another woman to be, if not the cause of this whole mess, certainly a factor.

Tilly squeezed my shoulder gently, letting me know I wasn't alone, before slipping quietly from the room, murmuring she would be outside keeping a lookout. I nodded silently.

Clutching the items I had been touching on the bed, I went to the bathroom. Pushing the door open, I couldn't help but smile at the beauty products and haircare paraphernalia strewn about, and more tears fell, finding their familiar path down my cheek. Toothpaste oozed from its tube and had formed a small, gelatinous peak on the basin – perhaps the maid hadn't been as thorough as I thought. I longed to be part of this chaos but knew I had to wait; my time would come.

Turning, I replaced the pyjamas to their place on the pillow, and the hair comb I had been fiddling with to the top of the pile on the bed, reminding myself that nobody could know I had been in the room. Walking to the door, I made a mental note of the extension number. Tilly passed a scribbled note to me just before the door closed and I placed it on the jam, hoping it wouldn't be missed.

Silently, we made our way to the ground floor and to the coffee shop. I sat, staring blankly, trying to organise my thoughts and feelings whilst Tilly returned the key to Romano.

I was unaware of my friend's return until a cup of coffee, and an accompanying miniature bottle of bourbon, were placed in front of me.

"Thought you might need this," Tilly said softly. A silence fell as we both gained our composure.

"They're here. My children are staying there, in that room." I was relieved and heartbroken all at once, and it was some time before Tilly spoke.

"Now, what we need to do is keep track of them. The note I left asked them to call me, or my room, to leave a message. I'm going to try and tie them up as much as possible until you're ready to make your move. I'll speak to their father and see what he has to say, though if I know men, which I think I probably do, he'll be extremely grateful to have them off his hands for a while." I listened to my friend's idea and knew what she was saying was true. What she was proposing was an excellent idea, if it worked.

"'Tilly, I can't begin to thank you for all you've done, and still are doing for me. I don't want you to tie yourself up in my affairs and jeopardise your own position – I would never forgive myself if you lost your job because of me," I said, bottom lip beginning to tremble again.

"Julia, if I'd known the situation from the beginning, I would have helped you back then. You have something very precious, and the person you trusted most is threatening to take that away from you. I'm your friend and it's my duty to do as much as I can to help you. It's what being a friend is all about." She looked deep into my eyes, as if willing me to understand the words she was saying.

"I'll forever be in your debt," was all I could reply. We sat quietly, drinking the coffee and whiskey, sun slowly descending on the horizon. I was lost in memories of the past, the happy times I had shared with my daughters. Tilly was quiet, as if lost in thought. She stood, suddenly.

"I'm going to go to my room now and check my messages. Then get changed. We, my dear, are going out to dinner, no arguments."

15.

I sat for some time alone and was beginning to feel a little better; it had been such a shock to see the room where Phoebe and Alice were staying, to see everything looking so natural and normal. Smiling to myself, I wondered how Mike was coping, having to organise two very excited females trying to make their mark in an environment made only to excite, enthral and entertain.

I was sure Tilly's plan would work but felt incredibly guilty for allowing her to shoulder so much responsibility on my behalf. Again, thinking of Mike, I couldn't help but laugh aloud, knowing he must be about ready to throw in the towel by now. He'd have been to every clothes shop, twice, and eaten in every fast food restaurant from one end of International Drive to the other – he must have spent a fortune. I thought briefly about money and where Mike's was coming from, but decided not to contemplate that side of things too much. I still fought with the notion of waiting in the room and taking the girls as soon as they stepped inside; that's what I wanted to do, but I knew it would only upset and confuse the girls, adding to the oncoming misery they were going to have to face.

Let them enjoy their holiday, I thought. There may not be another for a long while, and now that I felt I had people looking out for them, as well as me, I could wait. I walked along the path that led to my room, enjoying the warmth the early evening had to offer and began to feel more positive than ever. I allowed myself to smile; things were finally beginning to happen.

Sinking into a hot bath, I gave serious thought to my situation and what my plans would be on returning to England. There was still the job offer from the boarding school, but I was still unsure if it would suit our circumstances – there was, after all, nothing normal for Phoebe and Alice about having your mother at your school all day, and that was the main goal: normality. I had a suspicion that the offer had been made from sympathy and, though kind, perhaps wasn't the greatest reason.

I had grown a great deal stronger over the last few days and knew I could survive alone, something I would never have believed before now. My ability to think and make decisions for myself hadn't disappeared over the years, merely laid dormant. Being married to someone as successful Mike meant I'd had no need for these qualities. The only decisions I had to make were what to wear, when to book the next hair appointment and what time the children needed collecting from school.

Thinking of Mike made me feel angry and betrayed, but most of all, I was just sad. He was far more devious than I could've ever imagined, and I knew to win this fight I had to be devious too, only twofold. It was a small price to pay. There was also the recognition that I no longer loved my husband. I was unable to pinpoint the exact time this conclusion had been reached, but it was painful, nonetheless. The more thought I gave to the situation, the more I realised we had been spending months, possibly years, just going through the motions of married life.

Was it the same for him? I wondered. Had he been pretending, unable to make the hard decision until suddenly, it had been made for us? The events that had taken place left no choice but for action – but at what point had Mike decided to leave me, to sell the house? I still couldn't understand how he'd been able to hide his deception from Alex, from me. Despite my admission that there was no love for Mike, there was still the hope he hadn't become involved with anybody else, at least not yet anyway. Our daughters were going to have enough to try and cope with, and a girlfriend wouldn't help matters. I knew that, in time, this would be inevitable, but I hoped that Mike would allow them some breathing space first, some time to adjust.

Towelling myself dry after noticing my fingers were decidedly wrinkled, and the water cold, I hoped Tilly had good news and offered up a silent prayer that Mike had agreed to let Alice and Phoebe accompany her on the next few excursions.

As I left the room, I noticed it was cooler than it had been earlier and I was grateful I had bought a jacket. Tilly looked her usual, well-dressed self, wearing jeans, a red shirt and cowboy boots – she looked more American than the Statue of Liberty herself. I was always surprised at how unaffected my friend was at the constant stream of admiring glances and appreciative remarks that came her way.

As I walked further into the bar and my eyes adjusted to the light, I recognised Paul and caught his eye. He smiled and beckoned me to join him. Tilly was chatting animatedly to a group of people and hadn't yet noticed my arrival. I was suddenly very conscious how busy the bar was and hoped my husband and daughters were not in the near vicinity before remembering the US drinking laws, and I relaxed a little. Nobody under the age of twenty-one was allowed to drink alcohol and they preferred that children not even be on the premises. I almost felt as if I shouldn't even be here, like I was letting my children down by being somewhere you went for fun and relaxation – I was only here to find my children and go home, and I felt the guilt weighing heavy.

***

Paul saw Julia in the doorway. She always seemed to him to look pensive, never quite at ease. He found her incredibly attractive; her blonde hair, slightly tousled, and dark green eyes that seemed to bore straight into your soul. Yet, there was clearly something bothering her, a continuous weight on her mind that caused a slight frown, and he'd noticed a shadow would sometimes cross her face, clouding her beauty a little.

There was more to her story than the wish to become a travel rep, but she was too closed off to let anybody in. She had, however, appeared to have connected with Tilly and it seemed they were getting quite close. He had attempted to get her to open up a little the other evening when he had joined them for dinner; she had been a bit more relaxed, so he had tried to get to know a little more about her, but she'd shut him out instantly, politely but firmly.

***

As I approached, I smiled at Paul and when I was closer, he casually slipped his arm around my shoulders.

"What would you like to drink, Julia?"

"Scotch and soda please, Paul. Busy day?" I moved just enough so that his arm was no longer around me. As I waited patiently for my drink, I watched Tilly chat to people in the group, still unaware of my presence.

"Here's your drink." Paul smiled gently as he passed the half-filled tumbler.

"Thank you, Paul." I took the glass and returned my attentions to the group, occasionally scanning the remainder of the room to make sure Mike hadn't crept in. I felt Paul watching me.

"Have you plans for dinner?" He sounded casual, if not a bit nervous.

"Yes, Tilly and I are having dinner tonight," I said, using a tone that suggested the date was just for two.

"That's nice, perhaps I can join you both before your trip ends?"

I felt guilty; it was obvious he was only being friendly. I noticed, not for the first time, that he wasn't an unattractive man. I recalled what Tilly had said about him mentioning the photo – was he just being nosey, or was he trying to be helpful? I had no intention of trying to find out, though I did feel rude about my tone when I spoke to him.

"That would be lovely, Paul." I tried to make up for my earlier coldness.

Tilly, having finished her conversation, came up to the side of the bar where we were standing. Smiling her hello, she briefly chatted to Paul about alterations to the excursion timetables and then turned her attention to me.

"Ready to go and eat?"

"Ready when you are." I still wasn't at all hungry, but she'd done so much to help that I couldn't be rude; it was only dinner. I had noticed my clothes were hanging loosely – I'd lost some weight, hardly surprising, considering.

"Good, then let's go."

I said goodbye to Paul, and thanked him again for my drink, still feeling a little ashamed of my behaviour. He really was very attractive, and his smile made me feel self-conscious, awkward. I scolded myself for thinking in such a way, reminding myself that this was no way to behave; I was here for my children, nothing more. I followed Tilly out of the bar who must have seen or heard my reaction towards Paul judging by her next words.

"He's concerned about you. I think he suspects something is troubling you. Maybe you should let him help us."

"No, definitely not." I didn't mean to be snappish, but I didn't want any more people involved. I couldn't allow another person to take chances on my account – the guilt I felt was quite enough, I didn't need any more. "I'm sorry, I didn't mean to snap."

"Hey, no problem. Oh, by the way, we have cause for celebration," Tilly said, a mischievous smile tugging at her lips.

"We do?" I questioned, disbelievingly.

"We most certainly do. I spoke to your husband, and he was more than happy for your daughters to be included on some more day trips. In fact, he was positively enthusiastic. Phoebe and Alice told him what a good time they had had at Universal – he's just grateful to keep them occupied; they've apparently run him ragged," Tilly laughed.

"Oh, Tilly, that's marvellous! When's the next trip?"

"I happened to have scheduled them on one every day for the next four days. That leaves the fifth day free for you to make your entrance."

"Well, at least it keeps them here in Orlando. I can keep myself busy for four days, I'm sure." I didn't sound too convincing.

"I've been thinking about that, too," Tilly said, fidgeting. "There's a group of holidaymakers going to Clearwater for a few days. I think it would do you some good to get away, and Paul could always do with an extra pair of hands." She waited, biting her lip.

"Oh no, I don't think that would be a good idea. It's not fair on you, having to babysit my children as it is, and what if you need me? Plus, I don't think it's appropriate for me to be gallivanting around the seaside with somebody else right now."

"You would hardly be gallivanting around – you would be a trainee travel representative. It would be excellent experience for you. You'll get a good idea if this job is actually something you might really be interested in," added Tilly, obviously referring to my ruse. "Furthermore, you're better off away from here, anyway. It's not as if I can call you if the girls have a toothache or something – you're not supposed to be here, remember?" She had a point.

"What if Paul takes it the wrong way and thinks I'm there with him for other reasons?" I knew I sounded churlish, but I couldn't help myself. Deep down, I knew this was highly unlikely; he'd demonstrated a very professional attitude towards me thus far.

"Julia, give him some credit. He's hardly likely to jump your bones as soon as the opportunity arises. Though I'm sure if I asked him nicely, he might." Tilly was teasing now, and I laughed.

I thought about the suggestion as we drove to the steak house, which wasn't too far away. I had to admit, it was a logical idea, and the more I thought about it, the more I thought it could be a good idea. I still felt I shouldn't be indulging in anything other than searching for my children, but well, they'd been found now and all that was left for me to do, was wait.

"Okay, okay, let's do it."

Tilly whooped like a seasoned cowgirl.

***

Paul had been sitting in the coffee shop's outdoor terrace, waiting to make sure they got back safely and was pleased to see that they looked like they had enjoyed a pleasant evening together. He wanted Julia to be happy; on the odd occasion when she smiled, truly smiled, she looked even more beautiful. He may not know any details, but he felt Julia hadn't had much happiness recently; he only wished it was him, that could change that.

He watched them let themselves into their rooms and then took himself off to bed. He'd been tired, but the desire to see Julia safely back at the hotel had been overpowering.

***

Whilst I was letting myself into my room, I wasn't sure, but thought I had seen the shadowy figure of Paul, watching for me. For the first time in what seemed like an age, I felt safe as I undressed and fell into bed.

16.

It was a few minutes before I registered the ringing of the phone beside me, and I blearily raised my head. A splitting pain followed the slow movement. There was a dull ache at the back of my neck and my mouth felt dry, like I'd eaten sawdust. I didn't think I had drunk that much, but maybe in this climate you didn't need to; hangovers came easily. Fumbling with the receiver and trying to coax my mouth to work correctly, I mumbled what could have passed as a greeting.

"Hello, sleepyhead. I believe you'll be joining me this afternoon taking a group of sixty-somethings to Clearwater for a few days, excited?" Paul sounded far too chirpy for the time of day; quietly I cursed those who dared be morning people before looking at the clock, and wincing.

"Oh god, Paul, I'm sorry. What time is it, anyway?" I tried to sound as if I didn't know, hoping the delaying tactic would allow me time to reshuffle my brain into gear.

"It's precisely eight thirty in the morning, my dear," Paul said, chuckling.

"Must you sound so joyful?" I was slightly amused now.

"When I have just found out that I am being accompanied by a gorgeous woman, to a beautiful place for four whole days, what do you expect?" he teased.

"Well, ten out of ten for effort. When did you talk to Tilly?" I wished I'd had the opportunity to ask Paul myself, feeling I was enough of an imposition already without needing people to do the imposing for me.

"About seven thirty this morning – we had breakfast together before she started organising today's adventures." He was enjoying having the upper hand, I could tell by his tone.

"Has she already left?" I felt awful; I should have at least thanked her again for offering to take care of Alice and Phoebe. For an instant, I felt nervous about leaving the care of my children to Tilly – what if she had another incident and had to leave them? – before scolding myself; Tilly had more than proven herself and I knew I was being unfair.

"Just, but she left her mobile number so you can contact her whenever you like." Paul sounded so reassuring that I calmed a little. "If you like, we could meet for coffee and go over what we do on these little jollies. Does eleven sound okay?"

"That sounds great, Paul, I'll see you in the coffee shop." I put the receiver back in its cradle and lay in the warm bed. My mind was racing, fleeting thoughts of my daughters, husband and my friends, old and new, all of which culminated in a monumental headache.

Popping three headache pills, I headed for the shower. By eleven, I was suitably dressed and sitting in the coffee shop. The hotel laundry system had proven invaluable and I now had enough clean clothes to last the rest of the stay. Having checked my funds however, I knew I would have to start cutting back a little. Considering what I might be doing for the next few days, I thought that might not be too difficult.

Begrudgingly, I admitted I was looking forward to working, or at least helping out, instead of trying to keep myself occupied all the time. Once more, I thanked my lucky stars for Tilly. If not for her, I would never have gotten this far and I made a promise to do something nice for her before I left America.

My pulse quickened as I saw Paul making his way towards me, and I once again reprimanded myself; I was a grown woman in the middle of a crisis, not a bloody school girl with a crush. His dark hair caught the sunlight that filtered through the canopy of the coffee shop's terrace. He was obviously a man who was very much at ease with himself, casually acknowledging people on passing.

As he made his way through a group of children, choosing drinks from the cooler and passing the patisserie counter, I realised he was actually a little older than I had first guessed. His eyes were slightly lined, not adding weariness, but showing easy laughter and a love of life. Eventually, after chatting to the children for a few moments, he pulled up a chair opposite me and sat down.

"Well, well, how's the dirty stop out feeling?" Blue eyes dancing and grinning mischievously, he looked at me so intently that I was grateful for the tinted glasses I was wearing.

"I'm fine, thank you," I said primly, trying desperately to sound truthful.

"Well, I have to say – you look better than Tilly did this morning."

"She deserves a medal, having to put up with me and then doing a full day's work."

"She thinks a great deal of you and I'm sure you're not as bad as all that," he smiled.

I was beginning to feel a little more comfortable in Paul's presence. He didn't appear to want anything more than to be friends. The thought flitted through my mind before I laughed inwardly at myself; who would be interested in a woman the wrong side of thirty, who had nowhere to live and was on the brink of divorce, let alone one with two children –and teenagers at that?

Paul ordered more coffee for us and got down to the business, outlining the trip. As it transpired, there wasn't really a routine as such; the group we would be accompanying were all over sixty, and there were only twenty or so going. Most of the group consisted of couples who tended to do their own thing.

Paul and I would be just there in case they needed anything, and to make sure their rooms were satisfactory and organise transport. I quite liked the sound of the trip and agreed with Tilly; it would be excellent experience. Paul suggested we get our gear together and meet in the lobby in fifteen minutes.

"Oh, by the way, I forgot to ask you, Julia. What's your surname?"

Hesitating for a moment, I said, "Weston. Julia Weston."

Paul thrust his hand forward and stood to mock attention. "Well, Julia Weston, I know you know my name, but it's a pleasure to make your acquaintance," shaking my hand and smiling.

***

As Paul made his way back to his room, he knew he was bewitched by his new assistant. He had tried to find out more about her from Tilly, but she'd adamantly stated it wasn't her story to tell.

He knew she had experienced something traumatic and he even thought it might not be over yet, but whatever it was, she wasn't letting on. He decided he must be careful not to pry. He didn't want to scare her away.

***

At half past twelve, Paul and I rendezvoused as arranged. I was pleased to see Paul had only a small amount of luggage too, having had a horrible feeling we would have to dress for dinner every night, or be expected to sport a different swimsuit with every visit to the pool.

"Hello again," he said pleasantly, passing me a small holdall. "Tilly thought you might prefer to wear a uniform so you can feel the part. She also said that she guessed your size, so don't be surprised if you need to wear a belt the whole time."

I opened the bag and, sure enough, there was a blue skirt and jacket identical to my friend's, along with two white blouses. I inwardly shrugged; at least I would look official. We had a few minutes before the guests began arriving, so we went to the bar.

"Paul, I have to thank you for all of this. I promise I'll be as much help as possible and try not to get under your feet. You don't have to feel you need to keep me company all the time, I'm sure you will want to do..." I hesitated for a moment, before pushing forward. "Your own thing, and I don't want to get in your way." It sounded corny, even to me, but I felt better for having said it nonetheless.

Paul looked directly at me and threw his head back, laughing. Now I felt silly and he was *still* laughing.

"Whoa, just a minute, lady." His drawl made him sound like John Wayne and I stifled a giggle. "Just how old do you think I am?" I was confused, not really understanding what he was getting at. He continued,

"Julia, I am forty-two years old and don't get up to 'my own thing' as you so politely put it. Least of all while I'm working. If you think you might be cramping my style, I'm usually so exhausted after all the shepherding and chaperoning that the only style I have is the horizontal one." Realising the implication of his last statement, he added, "To sleep."

I was dumbfounded, there was no way the man sitting beside me now looked anywhere close to forty, and certainly not past it. There was no hint of grey in his hair, no swarthiness to his skin, but I did recall thinking earlier he might be older than I had first thought.

"Oh," was the only small sound to come from me as I took a sip from my drink. Feeling decidedly foolish, I was grateful for the elderly couple who intervened with a query, Paul leaving to sort out a lost luggage problem.

Ten minutes later, everybody was boarding the coach which would take us to Clearwater. In total there were only eighteen people going on the trip and they were all couples. They were a happy bunch, all excitedly choosing their seats and chatting away. Paul told me I would be sitting at the front with him. Once all the passengers were aboard, their luggage stowed, the driver started the engine and we pulled away onto International Drive. Paul did a quick headcount to make sure no one was missing.

Panic suddenly swept over me. I felt like I was abandoning my children; I had come all this way and had finally confirmed where they were, after all the tears, all the heartache, and now I was leaving them. I felt an all-consuming need to get off the coach and was about to shout for it to stop, when I felt Paul's hand on my arm. I was sweating and couldn't seem to catch my breath.

"It will be okay, I promise," was all he said, leaving his hand on my arm and looking directly into my eyes. I would never be able to explain why I instantly began to calm down, but I really did believe he might be right.

After a few minutes, my mind calmed and my breathing levelled again. I still felt emotional about leaving Orlando but had to tell myself I was only doing this for the benefit of my children. In the long term, I was ensuring that when we did finally depart, it was on the same schedule they already knew – I wanted everything had to be as structured as possible.

***

Paul was unnerved by how much he wanted to get to know Julia; she seemed to occupy almost every thought. It had been a long time since he had felt this way about anybody. He wished she wasn't quite so hostile, but knew he had to be patient. After chatting to a few of the couples on board he re-took his place next to her.

***

I had changed into the uniform Tilly had packed for me and felt a little more official; I was a different person now, with another role to fill, and it was almost therapeutic.

"I'm sorry for my little speech earlier. I'm just a bit nervous and don't want to be a burden to anyone," I explained simply.

"Julia, you're not a burden. In fact, you'll be great help and it's a pleasure to have you along." The sincerity with which he spoke made me smile.

"Oh, and another thing, you don't look bad for forty-two," I teased. Now he was smiling.

"Why thank you, ma'am." The drawl was even more pronounced. I didn't think I would ever tire of hearing him talk. The trip was only going to take a little under two hours and Paul and I managed to chat easily, though the conversation never drifted to anything personal I realised, as we reached Clearwater city limits, I knew almost nothing about Paul. I knew how old he was, and guessed he was American from his accent, but other than that, nothing. Similarly, he knew nothing about me and, for the moment, I decided it was safest that way, though my curiosity had been heightened.

There was silence as we took in the sights of the seaside town. Paul suddenly delved into his pocket and produced a piece of paper.

"I almost forgot, Tilly's number. She said to call anytime you like and she'll give you an update." I began to feel I might be able to trust this man. Not yet, but maybe soon. I unfolded the paper and looked at the number, making a mental note to give Tilly a call as soon as I was settled.

The coach crept slowly over the bridge that divided the downtown section of Clearwater from the beach and the numerous hotels, shops and restaurants that made up the district of Clearwater Beach. It was completely different to Orlando and I loved it already. We drove past the beach with its long stretch of beautiful golden sand. It was as warm as Orlando, but there was a delicious, gentle sea breeze. The coach finally came to a stop in the large car park of the Radisson Hotel and I became engrossed in helping the group disembark.

Most of the members of the group had been to the hotel on previous occasions and knew their way around. Paul had a chat with those who weren't familiar or needed a brief refresher as to the hotel's location and facilities. The entire group was given a leaflet, listing everything the hotel had to offer. There was a well-equipped gym on the top floor that was free of charge to all guests, and it also boasted three swimming pools and a private beach and jetty, which offered secluded sun bathing and dolphin watching. The two restaurants had bayside views and offered à la carte menus as well as buffet style lunch and breakfast.

I winced a little, thinking of my rapidly dwindling funds. Paul must have seen the expression on my face and informed the receptionist there was an extra under the tour operator's rate that was to be added to the company's invoice. I baulked and turned to Paul to dispute when he whispered,

"It's fine, little one, I promise you." Hearing Paul call me 'little one' made me feel slightly embarrassed, but it evoked a warm sensation in my chest. For a brief moment, there was another feeling I couldn't quite put my finger on. I wished I could sort out my emotions; they seemed to have a mind of their own and I wasn't sure I had control over anything right now.

Paul went back outside to organise porters for the luggage while I helped those who weren't quite sure where their rooms were. Taking my key, I noticed mine and Paul's rooms were next to each other.

The group agreed to meet again for dinner, allowing everybody time to settle in and explore and my bags arrived just as I was seeing the final couple to their room. I had to admit, I was quite enjoying my new role. Deciding to unpack later, I walked out into the glorious sunshine and warmth. Removing my jacket, I was grateful to Tilly for providing short sleeved shirts.

Across the road from the hotel was a small parade of shops, a miniature golf course made to look like a pirate's cove – complete with shipwreck, crocodiles and waterfalls – a petrol station, and a bakery. On the same side of the road as the hotel were more hotels and stunning condominium complexes, all rising high into the blue sky and having great views of the beach.

The beach itself was only a five- or ten-minute walk away. I'd never seen so many pelicans; some were snoozing on upright posts, others were diving for fish, many were just bobbing along on the gentle waves. The beach was busy with holidaymakers enjoying the sun, sea and sand. Taking off my shoes, I strolled to the water's edge. It was warmer than expected and the feeling of the gentle, lapping water against my toes was soothing. I smiled at the young children running in and out of the surf, tiny sun hats pulled onto their heads, buckets and spades in their hands, and in the next moment, I was crying. In my desperation I wondered if I should return to Orlando; at least I was closer to my children there. I calmed after a few minutes, knowing I would only have to hide away, and continued my walk.

Within an hour, I had walked as far as the splendid beachfront homes of the very wealthy. There weren't many people at this end of beach and I rested on a large rock close to the water's edge, staring out to sea for a moment, not thinking of anything, just being. The tension in my body was slowly beginning to ebb away, little by little.

As the sun began to set, looking like it was melting into the sea, I retraced my steps. The air had cooled as the sun went down, but only slightly, and people were now gathering to photograph the stunning display. Standing at the water's edge, I marvelled at the kaleidoscope of colours the sky became. Eventually, the deep purples gave way to dusk, signalling my return to the hotel.

Paul was in the lobby bar, enjoying a cocktail with a couple from the group. I was surprised to see he had changed from his blue and white uniform into chinos and a linen shirt. He smiled at me, beckoning to join him and his companions, and I pulled up a stool. Paul made the introductions and I chatted to the couple about their holiday. The couple finished their drinks and promised to meet up with Paul and me later for a nightcap. I once again felt self-conscious being solely in Paul's company. He offered another drink and I accepted, telling him about my walk and how much I loved Clearwater already. Paul explained he had been coming to the resort for the last eight years and thought of it as a second home.

"Did you go for a walk like that?" he asked, eyeing my uniform with amusement.

"Yes, I thought it was policy to wear the uniform during working hours," I stated defensively, annoyed with myself for being unable to stem the spreading colour of embarrassment I could feel rising across my face.

Apologising, Paul informed me that, strictly speaking, it was company policy to wear the uniform during working hours, but for some reason here in

Clearwater it wasn't necessary. He apologised once more for not telling me before now. Slowly, my tension subsided and agreed I could see how it may be more important in Orlando but that, here in Clearwater, it felt so relaxed that there wasn't as much need.

We sat and drank our drinks. Paul told me about his hometown in Arizona and it was fascinating to hear about his childhood, everything sounded so simple and wholesome. Life seemed to evolve around family. I managed to evade a lot of details about my own life. I was aware it was obvious and felt grateful he didn't push for more details. I began to think about Paul's age and wondered if he was married, having observed he wore no wedding ring – not that that offered any guarantees. He must have read my mind because he began to talk about his early married life.

"How old were you when you married?" I felt nosey for asking but couldn't help myself.

"Nineteen." He was staring into his glass, as if looking at an image only he could see.

"Wow, that was young," I said, before stupidly realising I had only been a year older myself when and Mike and I married. "Are you separated or divorced now?" Now I felt invasive and wished I had thought before opening my mouth. "I'm sorry, that's me just being nosey, forget I asked."

"No, I don't mind, it's just that I haven't thought much about Jessie in a long time." There was silence. I began to feel increasingly uncomfortable and could have kicked myself for being so intrusive.

"She died three years after we were married." The words were barely audible, and I gasped. "We were expecting our first child and she was killed in a car accident. They never caught the driver. Said he was probably so drunk he didn't even know he'd hit somebody." Paul's voice sounded distant, grief evident and my heart ached for him. I couldn't begin to imagine the pain he must have gone through. "So, that's when I decided to travel and ended up doing this job," he said, sounding brighter now. "It means I can get involved with children and, when that gets too much, I can spend time with the older generation and recharge my batteries." He was smiling again, and I was grateful.

"You never remarried?"

"Nope, never really had the inclination, but if that's an offer I could be persuaded." He was teasing again, and I laughed before checking my watch.

"Sorry, Paul, I'd like to ring Tilly and get changed. Do you want to meet for dinner?" I surprised myself with the question.

"Sure, how about back here at eight thirty? We'll make sure everybody is okay and we can go sample one of the local restaurants."

"Sounds great, I'll see you then."

The room was nicer than the one in Orlando and the bathroom had a sunken tub. Turning the taps and adding bubble bath, I went to the bedside cabinet and took out Tilly's number from the drawer. The phone rang just once at the other end before it was answered.

"Well, you took your time." Tilly was in a good mood and sounded pleased I had called.

"Sorry, Tilly, time flew so quickly. I did mean to call sooner. Paul is being a perfect gentleman and I'm sure my two darling daughters are driving you mad by now." The dull ache of loss hit me again. I felt a piece of me was missing and had been for so long now.

"Your daughters have been absolute angels. In fact, I have recommended they be put on the payroll. They've helped me keep the tiny tots amused at Typhoon Lagoon today and they're joining me at SeaWorld tomorrow. They're with their father now, who's apparently been playing golf all day." Tilly sounded pleased with herself. "I'm also pretty certain they won't be moving on anywhere else; they've asked your husband if they can stay at the hotel until they have to go home. He seems glad to have time to himself, so I think he's pretty happy to indulge them."

"Have they mentioned anything about me?" I knew it sounded pathetic, but I felt so shut out that I couldn't help myself.

"Only that they missed you, and hoped you were better now." I felt happy and angry all at once – I was happy that they missed me, but angry for the picture Mike had painted. As far as I knew, he could have told them I was a basket case and needed locking up. I knew

I may be exaggerating slightly, a little melodramatic, but didn't care.

"Thanks again, Tilly. I feel like that's all I ever say to you, but I promise I'll make this up to you."

"I'll not hear another word of it."

"I'll call you again tomorrow, is that okay?"

"Same time, same place," Tilly said, before hanging up.

Sinking into the hot bubble bath, I allowed my mind to switch off and the soft fragrance of the scented water to soothe my body and soul. Taking time to towel myself dry before smoothing body lotion over my warm skin, I felt quite calm and, at last, like I had some control over the situation. It wouldn't be long now before I was able to take them home or, at the very least, back to their school. I was pleased that their lives would still contain a degree of normalcy; they'd boarded for a time when they were younger, back when I would often accompany Mike on his business trips. All other aspects of our lives, however, had changed beyond all recognition.

Dressing simply in jeans and a white shirt, I allowed my hair to fall loosely around my shoulders, not having to keep it tied up now I was no longer in Mike's immediate vicinity. I applied only a touch of make-up, my surroundings making me feel the natural look appropriate.

It was early but I felt confident enough to go to the lobby bar anyway. Ordering a dry martini, I sat, watching a pod of dolphins in the bay stage a free show for anybody who cared to watch. I marvelled at the twists and jumps the dolphins were executing, simply because they could, in no hurry to end their performance.

I felt Paul's presence before my gaze fell upon him. I was hardly able to believe how every encounter with this man made me feel like a nervous schoolgirl. I extended my hand and realised it was somewhat too formal a gesture – I seemed to lose all common sense around him. Paul merely accepted my hand, bent at the hip and lightly kissed it, before bowing once more theatrically.

"Good evening, madam." His mock English accent was awful. "Glad to see you're enjoying the show I commissioned, especially for you." He motioned to the dolphins still jumping and swirling in earnest.

"You really are a remarkable man." I decided to play along. "Is there nothing you can't do?"

"Your wish is my command, m'lady."

"In that case, I wish for another dry martini."

All accents dropped, and he adopted his usual drawl. "Consider it done," he said, before turning towards the bar. I felt the stirring of something long forgotten and I, again, gave myself a stern talking to. Attraction should be the last feeling I should be entertaining right now. I switched my attention back to the bay, figuring it was the safest option.

The dolphins had gone, and there was serene silence as the stars began to make their appearance in the sky. I watched couples sitting on the deck outside enjoying the intimacy the night sky offered, sitting close and talking in hushed tones to each other, sharing private thoughts and wishes. Loneliness threw its dark cloak around my shoulders. Paul silently placed my drink before me.

***

Her mind was clearly elsewhere. He marvelled at the colour and lustre of her hair, the soft spun gold gently softening the angular contours of her face. Unusually dark lashes framed her dark green, almond shaped eyes. It wasn't the first time he had wondered why such a beautiful woman was alone.

"Here's your drink." He felt like he was intruding, and the words sounded dumb.

"Thank you." Julia's voice was quiet and sad.

"So then, how about I show you the local sights? First, we go eat at a restaurant I know, and then I'll give you a quick tour of the homes of the rich and shameless." He smiled, hoping to cheer her up

"That sounds great." She seemed to relax at his words and Paul was grateful for the mood change. It broke his heart to see this amazing woman so sad. He knew he was falling in love and could do nothing to stop it. He wasn't sure he wanted to.

***

We had dinner at the Rockaway Grill, casual dining right on the beach. I was enjoying the crab salads served in half pineapples, and the tuna burgers were amazing – I surprised herself as to how much I ate. Must be the sea air, I reasoned.

All courses were washed down with ice-cold beer, straight from the bottle. Conversation came easily and the time flew by. I was astounded at how many countries Paul had visited. Wherever he went though, he had never felt able to settle, always feeling there was something else to see, something new to experience. He said he'd travelled for over three years, almost non-stop, before coming to the conclusion that what he'd been searching for wasn't a place – at least, not in the physical sense – but rather, somewhere where he could be happy. Once he'd realised that, he'd returned home.

It was late when we finally returned to the hotel. I kissed Paul lightly on the cheek and thanked him for a lovely evening. Taking the elevator to our floor, I knew Paul wasn't the predator I had initially taken him for – he hadn't accompanied me, saying he had a few things he wanted to go over with the hotel before retiring.

I didn't realise how tired I was and fell asleep the instant my head hit the pillow. My last thought before the darkness took me was of the calming, rhythmic sound of the surf and the comfort I felt, knowing where my children were at last.

17.

Dawn broke way to the sound of gulls calling and pelicans beating their wings, as if in some way trying to cool themselves down already. I had spent another night fighting the nightmares – when I'd been able to sleep at all – and the feeling of guilt, when awake. I'd sat in the dark staring out to sea, watching the light of the moon dance across the gentle waves. I had felt annoyed with my behaviour the previous evening; what was I thinking? My children were still out there, in the world without me, and I'd wasted precious time on frivolous pursuits with Paul.

I knew I was lucky to have a friend looking out for them, but even that was no guarantee all was well. There was still nothing to say Mike wouldn't change his mind and whisk them off somewhere else. Tilly couldn't force him to leave the girls in her care, and I had no idea what his plans were. I hated the complete lack of control over the situation I had. I felt miserable, feeling sick to my stomach. Maybe I should have just grabbed them and ran and dealt with the consequences of doing so later, but I knew I would have regretted doing that to my children. It would have made me no better than their father.

Knowing I had to put on a brave face, my day began. The day took a relaxed routine; I walked with a small group as far as I had gone the previous day and tried to keep cheerful. The members of my group took great pleasure in fantasizing about how wonderful it must be to live in the beachfront houses, all making promises that if they ever had a windfall, they would buy such a property. I thought that, under different circumstances and if I ever had the means, I also would love to return to Clearwater, living as close to the sea as possible.

The day passed, too slowly in my mind, but everyone else seemed to have enjoyed themselves. When I finally met up with Paul, he was busy with a couple who wanted to change their room but was unsatisfied with the alternative offered. By late afternoon, the couple had been offered a room with a private balcony and were finally happy. He joined me and another couple for coffee, where we were enjoying the view from the deck.

"You're looking better; you're even getting a suntan!"

I blushed at his comment. "Thanks," I smiled weakly, aware of our company and wanting to give the right impression. My emotions continued to see-saw, swinging from elation to despair, and I felt close to collapse. The elderly couple excused themselves, explaining that they were going to their room for a nap and left us together on the deck.

"Julia, why are you here in America?"

The question came from nowhere and threw me. Thinking for a moment, I considered repeating the travel rep story before thinking better of it, feeling, finally, I could trust Paul. He had helped me when he had no reason to and last night, he had opened up to me about his past – it was only fair to reciprocate. I was nervous, but decided to take the risk.

Beginning with the events in England, Paul listened silently. I told of how I had discovered my children had been taken and how that had led to me coming to Florida. Telling of my deceit to Tilly, which still embarrassed me, he offered no recrimination. I finished with my reasons for coming to Clearwater, at Tilly's suggestion, and once again thanked Paul for allowing me to tag along, apologising if I had, in any way, become a burden. I admitted having never considered doing a job like this but, after experiencing it a little, feeling as though I may one day take it further.

Paul had listened without interruption and hadn't passed any judgment. I felt uncomfortable as silence fell between us. I wondered if Paul thought he had got himself tied up with some neurotic female, and was planning an escape. Was he going to send me back to Orlando? I wasn't sure I cared if he did, the darkness of depression beginning to take hold for what felt like the hundredth time.

"I'm going to help you in any way I can, I promise." The words made me jump, not expecting the response, or the conviction I could hear behind it.

"Thank you, Paul, but I think this is my battle and I don't want to drag any more people into it."

"You need all the help you can get. Tilly has proved herself a friend in the very truest sense of the word and I also would like to count myself as a friend to you." The sincerity in his words and voice made my eyes shine with fresh tears. Unable to stem their flow, I reached for my handbag for a tissue – why did I have to cry every time I was showed kindness? Paul offered his handkerchief and I almost laughed out aloud at the absurdity of a man like Paul, looking as though he had just stepped out of a western movie, having a freshly laundered handkerchief to hand.

"Do you know where your daughters are today?" he asked, his voice expressing concern.

Smiling and looking at my watch, I replied, "I would say that, by now, they've driven Tilly, or some other poor soul, mad and are about to be leaving for SeaWorld."

Paul laughed. "Why didn't you tell me all of this sooner?" He was gentle in his questioning.

"When your world is turned upside down within the space of twenty-four hours, and you've experienced the kind of betrayal I have by the person you trusted most, you shut off from trusting anybody. I admit, it's not always the best way to deal with a situation, but I couldn't bring myself to trust and then be hurt again. But the stakes are too high now. All I want to do is take my children home, pick up the pieces as best I can and move on with life." I had to stop talking, I didn't want give in to the tears.

"You say you've no friends or family at home, no one that can help you when you return?'

"The only friend I thought I had was Marcia, and she hasn't contacted me at all since the business was seized."

"Some friend!" I winced at the bitterness in Paul's voice.

"I can't really blame her; she doesn't know any better. She's just a product of her parents and the society she knows."

"You are far too forgiving, but maybe that's what makes you a survivor." He spoke the words gently as he wiped away the tears that seemed to continue regardless, leaning across the table to softly kiss my forehead. "Don't cry, little one. It's going to be all right; I promise."

The warmth from where his lips had been spread through my body. I had the feeling of being wrapped in a soft blanket, feeling safe.

"On a brighter note, shall we eat local-style, or would you prefer to have a more sophisticated meal this evening?" Paul was trying desperately to cheer me up.

"Oh, local please. Besides, my wardrobe doesn't stretch to sophistication." I managed to laugh, still wiping away tears.

"Lady, you could wear a paper bag and still look sophisticated." The deepness of his voice made my heart beat loudly, and I was sure he must know the effect he had on me.

"Can I just go and freshen up? I want to give Tilly a call." It was that time of day again, and it gave me a moment to gather my composure.

"Sure thing, how about we meet back here in about an hour?"

I kissed his cheek and thanked him for listening. It felt the most natural thing to do, but I still surprised myself by doing it.

***

Paul sat for a while, thinking about what Julia had told him. She had been through so much. He wanted to protect her, to stop the pain, but he knew he had to let her get her children back in her own way. He vowed he was going to be there for her though, knowing for sure he was in love with her. At first, there was guilt, the memory of Jessie still fresh, but he thought she'd understand – Jessie would have been happy for him.

***

I washed my face, feeling relieved to have told Paul, but now terrified of my feelings towards him; there was an intensity to him, so visceral it almost frightened me. Yet, there was a gentleness as well, one I had never before witnessed. Changing my skirt and combing my hair, I studied my face in the mirror. The person staring back wasn't the same person of almost two weeks ago. This one was real; flawed, yes, one who had been hurt beyond belief, but a fighter nonetheless. I was actually beginning to like myself.

I counted the minutes leading up to when I could call Tilly. I had to stop myself from dialling the number, my anxiety peaking as the day wore on. The time came and the phone was answered on the second ring. Relief flooded through me; even now, I felt uneasy, as if my plan would go wrong in some way. I spoke about my conversation with Paul and Tilly seemed pleased I had finally confided in him. I didn't mention my feelings towards him though, still unsure of them myself.

"How were Phoebe and Alice today?"

"They were great. They're so helpful and I think they had a good day – they were pretty tired out when we got back to the hotel though."

"They didn't cause you too much trouble?" I was still concerned with the imposition I was putting on my friend.

"Trouble, hardly!" she snorted before continuing, "I wonder how I ever coped without them, the other kids love them."

I was pleased they were enjoying themselves; it was their holiday, after all, and it made the separation a little easier to bear.

"Just one more day in sunny Clearwater and you'll be back here, ready to make your appearance and take them home." Neither of us mentioned the inevitable confrontation between Mike and I.

"So, where to tomorrow?" I asked. Tilly had told me her itinerary for the whole stay, but still felt the need to check and re-check every aspect.

"Gatorland, but I'm waiting to hear back from the girls to see if they can join us." My heart froze. What if Mike said they couldn't go, had other plans to take them away? The voice inside my head was screaming the questions.

"Do you think there might be a problem?" I tried to sound calm.

"No, I think your daughters have your husband wrapped around their little fingers," Tilly replied, sounding slightly uneasy. "I'll speak to you tomorrow though – don't worry."

***

Paul made me laugh so much that night that my sides ached; he made me feel alive again. My anxiety had eased slightly with the help of Paul's reassurance and I decided being optimistic and positive were the best qualities to adopt – they were virtues I had always suggested my children live by, and I should probably follow my own advice. Paul was terrific company and I felt we had a lot in common; we had both lost things dear to us in life. I, however, had been given a chance to recover the most important parts of my loss and for that, I knew I should be grateful.

As the night wore on, I felt a gentle flow of feelings long-forgotten and, letting them come freely, I kissed Paul with pent-up passion. He returned with a fervour I had never experienced before, and we kissed until we were breathless. Silently, I led him by the hand to my room, guiding him inside.

"Are you sure this is what you want?" he asked huskily, his longing evident.

"Paul, this is most definitely what I want." Suddenly anxious, I nervously asked, "You want it too, don't you? Oh, god, am I being too forward? This is not something I make a habit of, I promise."

Paul laughed and pulled me towards him. I barely came to his shoulders and could feel the heat of his body. I ached with longing.

"You, my dear, are a woman who knows what she wants. Enjoy it, use it."

Slowly, nervously, I undressed him, feeling his every muscle tense as my fingers felt their way over his body. I heard his breath quicken and my excitement heightened. He, in turn, unbuttoned my shirt and let it fall to the floor. I was wearing nothing underneath and my nipples instantly hardened.

He knelt before me, removing my boots and jeans. His appreciation of my body was evident, and I felt my own needs soar in response. Pulling me down onto the bed with a lust that made me gasp, our bodies became one almost instantly. Our climaxes rose, one long, simultaneous fire that burned bright and powerful enough to eventually render us silent. I had never felt a hunger like I felt for the man beside me, nor could I ever recall being so satisfied by sex. Yet, I instantly felt the need for more. It was like he was a drug and I, an addict. As my hunger rose, the soft cloak of sleep shrouded me and I gave in to its velvet touch. For the first time in a very long time, I slept soundly.

Waking to the sound of the surf once more, I opened my eyes, knowing Paul was there, the warmth from his body washing over me. Slowly, so as not to wake him, I manoeuvred myself to face him, basking in his scent. I couldn't believe my behaviour of the previous night, my emotions swinging wildly from deep shame and guilt, to feeling empowered, and even a little scared by my own desires.

"Sleepyhead, I think it's time we got up," I whispered into his ear. His eyes opened slowly, and he smiled at me.

"Morning, little one." Every time he called me that, my heart skipped a beat, now accompanied by the stirrings of desire.

"What's the time?" he asked, as he leant forward to kiss me.

"Almost nine," I smiled. Paul sat bolt upright.

"We had better get a move on, then."

We both began to get dressed, interrupting our haste to kiss, neither of us really wanting to hurry but knowing there were people expecting us. I felt the return of unease as I thought about my daughters. Had they gone with Tilly? I felt guilt for my actions for the previous night, but knew I had to accept the fact I had strong feelings for Paul. I noticed Paul looking at me and decided now wasn't the time to burden him with my fears.

Finally, we made our way to join the other guests in the dining room. I was hungry, and enthusiastically helped myself to the breakfast buffet. Looking up briefly, I noticed a number of eyes watching. The elderly couples were smiling knowingly in both mine and Paul's direction.

"Have we got signs on our backs, or something?" I whispered to Paul.

"Well, we do look a bit too happy," he laughed, looking at me with adoring eyes.

"Oh well. So be it." I didn't care anymore and neither, it seemed, did Paul.

Paul had some business to attend to, which meant he would be unavailable for the day. This came with mixed blessings; I was still unsettled by my feelings, and for some reason I had a niggling sensation of contrition; had I betrayed Mike, my children? Could I really be guilty of betrayal, after everything he had done to me? I didn't know if engaging in a sexual encounter with another man, one who wasn't my children's father, was a betrayal of them. Confused, I was grateful for the time to try and sort through my emotions alone. As soon as he left, I missed him.

The rest of the morning was filled with the walk along the beach. It seemed I was constantly tormented by destructive emotions, never quite feeling I was where I should be. I knew I should be with my children, but had to accept that this would only come with time.

I had quite a following now; almost all our group joined me for the walk and we stopped for ice creams on the way back. I avoided watching children playing in the surf, their happy faces crushing my heart with longing. I needed to be stronger than ever, it was almost time. If I allowed myself to think much about Phoebe and Alice, I wanted to jump on the first bus back to Orlando and the waiting was excruciating.

There was a small shopping excursion and a little bit of sightseeing on Clearwater Beach's Jolly Trolley, which served as a distraction. I was able to avoid any in-depth conversations with the members of the group and the day wound down quicker than the previous one.

Throughout the day I felt a sense of abandonment, not my own abandonment, but a feeling that I had been guilty of abandoning my children. What if Tilly was reassigned to another trip? What if I had misjudged our friendship and I never heard from her again? What if Mike had changed his mind at the last minute or even changed his plans completely again? So many possibilities were running through my head, so much so that by the afternoon I was desperate to get some confirmation they were safe. Panic was beginning to flood my body.

As soon as I was back in the privacy of my room, I rang Tilly. She answered on the second ring and instantly confirmed Phoebe and Alice had joined her on the Gatorland excursion. I felt tears of relief stinging my eyes as Tilly told, in detail, of the day's adventures. I savoured every word, feeling closer once more to my missing children. I didn't tell Tilly about Paul. I would, just – not yet.

Dinner was at a restaurant close to the hotel, Leverocks. It had a huge glass front that allowed diners to watch the boats, jet skiers and, quite often, wild dolphins in the bay. Having wrestled with my emotions all day and beginning to feel trepidation at returning to Orlando, I wasn't really hungry. When Paul joined me, I was shocked at how much desire I felt for him as soon as I saw him. We ordered filet mignon and lobster tails, but ate very little. Instead, I drank three cocktails, which helped ease my tension and I relaxed a little. We talked about our day's events, the conversation easy and light-hearted, before joining the rest of the group back at the hotel for drinks.

It was the early hours of the morning before everybody began to turn in and, this time, we spent the night in Paul's room, making love until daybreak, never tiring of each other's passion. I surprised myself with my enthusiasm to take the lead and bring Paul to climax at my will. He, in return, skilfully brought me to orgasm for what seemed like a delicious eternity. There was something desperate about our love-making, as if it would be our last night together.

I couldn't help but be subdued the following morning. I was becoming increasingly nervous; I knew it had to be faced, but was still unsure as to the exact outcome.

Paul could tell, for all my bravado, that I was slowly beginning to clam up. The sky outside was heavy and grey, suggesting a storm was on its way, as if echoing the mood and the inevitable conflict.

***

Paul knew he and Julia needed to talk. He had come to a decision, and he needed Julia to hear it. Taking the table furthest away from the rest of the group who were chatting happily away to each other, they sat in silence for a moment, each content with the other's company.

18.

It was Paul who broke the silence.

"Little one, I need you to know something. I have some matters to sort out here in America..." I braced myself, expecting the 'it's been nice, but—' speech. I was just beginning to shut down, when I heard, "Then I'm coming to England." I couldn't believe my ears.

"What did you just say?" I asked, thoroughly confused.

"I said, I have a few matters to sort out here in America and then I am coming to England."

I didn't know whether to laugh or cry.

Paul continued, "There are some affairs I need to put in order that will probably take about a week, and then I'm coming to England to be with you. I think you're going to need time with your children, and I don't think my being around them straight away would be a good idea. They're going to have enough to deal with after tomorrow." He looked directly into my eyes. "I mean it, little one, I'm not leaving you – unless, of course, you don't want me. In which case, I'll just be your best friend until you do." He smiled boyishly at me and my heart melted.

The group had dispersed to do some last-minute shopping, or to laze around the pool until the coach was ready to take them back to Orlando. I didn't believe Paul at first, thinking he would just disappear once we were back in Orlando. He explained he had a property in Arizona he wanted to get on the market. I didn't ask, but guessed it was the home he had shared with his wife all those years ago. He also had some financial dealings he needed to work through.

Paul told me that when his wife had died, her insurance money was put into an account and left there, he was unable to bring himself to touch it. He now felt it had a purpose. Paul gave me a collection of phone numbers that meant he would be available to contact at any time, day or night. Once Paul had convinced me of his intentions, and I'd allowed myself to believe him, we planned to meet once back in England and just enjoyed our last few hours together.

Three o'clock came around all too soon and everybody boarded the coach. I felt the tension in my muscles grow, stiffening with anxiety. Paul sat beside me and squeezed my hand reassuringly. I was back in my travel rep uniform, my hair tied back in a ponytail, dark glasses covering my eyes. The closer we got to Orlando, the worse I felt. Finally, pulling into the car park of the Quality Inn Plaza, I was finding it hard to concentrate, my mind racing.

Tilly was standing outside, looking expectant.

"Hello, Julia." Tilly extended her arms and we hugged, I had missed her company. "I see you were well looked after,' she remarked, noticing my healthy glow, still apparent beneath my anxious expression.

I said hurried goodbyes to the group and Tilly steered me away to my room. I was worried about being spotted by Mike or the girls – I wasn't ready for them yet and was thankful Tilly had organised me a room.

"Where are the twins?" I asked, desperate to know they were still okay.

"It's okay, honey, they're fine. They managed to talk their father into taking them to King Henry's Feast tonight, so they should be jousting and clashing tankards with the best of them by now." Once more, I thanked my friend for all her help and felt a little calmer, knowing they were occupied elsewhere.

Tilly stayed whilst I showered and changed, sitting on the edge of the bed, waiting for me to re-emerge from the bathroom.

"So, how did you and Paul get along then, in Clearwater?" It was clear she was trying to make it sound as casual a question as possible. I came out of the bathroom, dressed and drying my hair.

"Oh, just fine thanks." I was teasing her, knowing she was desperate for news. I knew she'd been waiting to hear the gossip, and decided it wasn't fair to hold back from her any longer. I sat down on the bed beside Tilly, still drying my hair, making sure my face was obscured by the towel. I dropped the towel and faced my friend and smiled.

"Uh-oh," laughed Tilly. She looked at me. "I take it you two got on better than fine."

I told her the events of the last few days, and about Paul's wish to follow me to England. Tilly listened and looked delighted for both of us. We sat and chatted for hours, a pleasant distraction. The twins, according to Tilly, had planned on making the most of their last day in America with a day of lounging around the pool and topping up their tans, which gave me a backdrop against which to carry my plan. We hugged and said goodnight, promising to catch up at some point in the morning.

***

Tilly came across Paul in the hotel bar.

"Hi stranger."

Paul turned and smiled at her. "Hey Tilly, how goes it?"

"Just fine… more to the point, how are you?"

"Missing her already," he replied, sipping from his half-empty glass.

"You look like you lost a dollar and found a penny."

"Nope, but I do feel like I've lost the woman I love. I can only hope she believed me when I said I'm going to follow her." He sat, staring into the bottom of his glass. "I know I said I would stay away for a while, she has to do whatever it is she has to do, but it already hurts so much. A few nights together and I feel like I can't go on without her. I need to see her, feel her, smell her."

Tilly moved closer to her friend and hugged him.

"Just be strong for her, Paul. She's going to need all the strength we can give her; she's going to have to be so strong, for herself and for her children."

"I want to go and rip that man's throat out for hurting her like this," he spat, anger rising.

"I know, but we can't get involved, we can't scare him off. Right now, Julia knows where her kids are and that's all that matters." Tilly could see she was getting through to Paul. The pair sat and drank until late into the night, both hoping the next day would go well – it was Julia's turn now.

✝✝✝

Panic arose in me in time to the rising sun. It was only seven thirty and the humidity was as heavy as my heart. Today was the day I would confront Mike. Tonight, I would have my children with me and tomorrow I would take them home. There was no other outcome I would allow, though what would happen once back in England, I didn't know.

I wished it was tomorrow already, all the arguing and tears having been dealt with. The only way to get through this day would be to concentrate on seeing my daughters; I hadn't seen them for almost two weeks and my heart ached for them.

They may be teenagers, but they were still my babies. I never again wanted to feel my heart being torn to shreds, as it had when Mike took them away. My plan was to find them later that morning and spend as much time with them as possible. If Mike was with them, then I would just have to deal with that. In my mind, I realised I had to play things cool; the priority was to keep the girls calm, to not frighten them. There was still a very rough road ahead for them and, if I could help it, I didn't want to add anything more to it than was necessary.

Slowly, I showered and dressed, checking my money. I found I had spent considerably less than I had first thought in Clearwater, thanks to Paul. I could take the twins shopping if things went well. Not knowing how the day would end, I packed my bags. If necessary, I would be able to collect them and go, in a matter of minutes. Checking the whereabouts of my passport, tickets and the usual bits and pieces, I was satisfied I knew exactly where everything was.

Reading the information on the plane ticket, it advised to ring the day prior to departure to see if the flight schedule had changed. Picking up the phone, I dialled the number shown. It was a recorded message, confirming the departure time as being half past five in the afternoon, the following day. No changes. Replacing the receiver, I tried to imagine what life would be like by then, what events would have taken place. My imagination failed me. Eventually, I made myself have some breakfast, I wasn't hungry but I knew that to think straight, I needed to have something to eat.

Walking through the coffee shop, I couldn't help but look for Paul; there were very few people about, and he wasn't one of them. Finding my usual table, I ordered coffee and collected a plate from the buffet, piling it with eggs, hash browns and ham before returning to my seat. Hardly touching the food, I drank my coffee slowly. The twins wouldn't be awake yet. Smiling to myself, I wondered how they had managed to get up each morning when Tilly had included them on the excursions. At home, they rarely surfaced before eleven at the weekends. I had a feeling today they would have a lie-in.

My waiter noticed I had hardly touched my food and enquired if it wasn't to my liking. Smiling, I told him I wasn't as hungry as had first thought and instead, ordered more coffee. After sitting quietly, watching the steady flow of breakfasters come and go, I decided to have a wander around, to kill time.

Walking through the hotel lobby, I watched a group of tourists boarding their coach for the airport, going home. Watching them, I felt a strong pang of homesickness. I wished I was boarding that bus with my children. The sun was beating down in earnest and the heat was making the tarmac steam; before long, everywhere would be as dry as cinder again.

***

The hotel had three pools, two heated conventionally and the other by solar heating and although it took a while to reach temperature each day, this was actually the most popular pool. Alice and Phoebe had woken early and had decided to make the most of their last full day. They were already tanned from their recent daily outings, but decided you could never be too brown. They were convinced that, as soon as they got home, it would rapidly disappear, being almost gone by the time they went back to school on Monday.

Chatting loudly, they made their way across the steaming tarmac to the pool nearest their room. They were worried about their parents. Mummy, as they now knew, wasn't well. Daddy didn't go into much detail, but they knew she needed lots of rest and may be away for some time recovering. They had wanted to call her, wherever she was, but Daddy had said that under no circumstances were they to try, because it would upset her and then she wouldn't get better. They were confused by Daddy's behaviour; whilst they'd been here, he'd done nothing but snap at them one minute and then take them shopping for loads of new clothes and shoes the next.

He had made quite a few phone calls but was always just finishing them whenever they walked into the room. They assumed he must be talking to Mummy's doctors or something and were glad when he had let them go with Tilly to the theme parks. They had had such a great time. Tilly was so cool.

Opening the gate to the pool area, they found the sunniest spot and dragged a couple of white plastic sun loungers into the bright sunlight. Settling themselves down, one with a book, the other with an iPod, they switched off to the outside world.

*　*　*

I took the route around the back of the hotel to where the pools were, each accompanied by its own Tiki Bar, which was, in fact, nothing more than a concrete hut with coconut matting as its roof. The first pool was quite small and there was no one about, all the loungers neatly stacked, the previous day's rubbish collected long ago.

The second pool was in direct sunlight and the reflection from the water, even in the morning sunlight, was almost blinding. It wasn't until I walked closer to the fence surrounding the pool area that I noticed the two willowy figures on the loungers, side by side.

My heart began to race, my legs carrying me faster without realising it. All other sound and life had stopped, the earth no longer turning; there was only the vision before me. I threw open the gate. It was them. A sob escaped, and then another. I was almost on my knees before Alice and Phoebe noticed me, seemingly taking a moment to recognise me.

"Mummy!" they both cried, my arms already around them both, tears spilling freely down my face. The twins were crying too. Rapidly kissing the soft, fair hair of my daughters, I held them tight, unable to speak. The power of the emotions I was feeling struck me mute.

"Oh, Mummy, we're so glad you're here!" Alice was trying desperately to talk between sobs.

"Are you feeling better now?" Phoebe added, a shadow of concern spreading across her upturned, tear-stained face. Remembering what Tilly had told me, I decided to play along with the lie for the time being. I owed nothing to Mike, to help keep his story going, but felt it better for my children. They would know the truth soon enough.

"Yes, I'm fine," and then realising this sounded somewhat lame, I added, "how about you two? How have you been?"

The twins then gave me a full, detailed account of every single day of their stay. We sat, hugging each other, as I listened to them talk for each other, over each other, correcting each other, and I felt I could not love them any more than I did at that very moment. I rubbed the back of my hand over my eyes, tears relentlessly falling, whilst in my arms I held the two most precious things.

"Oh, Mummy, we've missed you so much," Alice said. "We're so glad you're better."

I didn't know what to say, hugging them closer still. What I wanted to say was that their stealing, deceiving, bastard of a father had stolen our home, money, livelihood and, in effect, his best friend's life and had also tried to steal them, my own flesh and blood. Instead, I said that I was with them, and that was all that mattered.

The girls stopped crying, but I found it impossible. I kept looking at my two beautiful daughters and knew how close I had come to losing them for good. Mike, I vowed, would pay. Alice turned to me with a quizzical look.

"Daddy doesn't know you're here, does he?"

"No, I thought I'd surprise him," I spoke quietly, not lying.

"But, Mummy, he's gone to play golf until lunchtime." Phoebe sounded devastated. I, on the other hand, was delighted.

"Don't worry, darling, he doesn't know I'm here, so we can just spend some time together and then surprise him when he comes back." He would be surprised alright, I thought darkly. This explanation seemed to satisfy them, and they left their loungers, linking arms with me, before walking to room 271 so they could get changed.

The room was no longer a shock to me. It was just a room where my daughters had slept. I paid no regard to where Mike was, knowing that would come later. Our happy threesome went shopping in the complex opposite the hotel where I had spent so much time, alone and desperate. This time, I knew the true meaning of happiness, and skipped across the pedestrian crossing with a daughter on each arm.

I bought the girls new roller blades and was almost talked into buying a pair for myself; fortunately for me, the shop didn't carry my size and the matter was dropped. We stopped for hot chocolate topped with huge spoonfuls of whipped cream, followed by enormous doughnuts covered in the stickiest sauce I had ever encountered, having to spend some time desperately trying to remove splashes of it from my face.

The time came when we had to start making our way back to the hotel. For a fleeting moment, I considered doing to Mike exactly what he had done to me, running off with my daughters. Almost as quickly, I knew it would make me no better than him and only serve to confuse and frighten my children. All they were aware of right now, was that their mother had joined them for the final day of their holiday and to surprise their father. It was clear to me that they had no inclination of any of the events that had transpired back in England.

I followed my daughters up the stairs to their landing. Between the three of us, we had far too much to carry, and were giggling as we each, in turn, dropped one or more of our parcels. Phoebe placed her key in the lock and turned the knob, door springing open with a gentle push, and we stepped into the room. My heart had started to pound loudly. I could see the light from around the bathroom door, Mike was here. The television was playing, its artificial glow making moving mosaics on the bedspread.

19.

"I'll be out in just a minute, girls." Mike's voice came from behind the bathroom door. I thought I heard the faint hum of an electric razor, then taps running. I was clammy, throat dry, my tongue feeling way too big for my mouth. The sound of my own heartbeat was deafening, pounding in my ears and beating at breakneck speed. I felt the compelling urge to run away and yet, didn't want to move a muscle at the same time; it was torturous. Phoebe and Alice giggled to themselves quietly, not wanting to spoil the surprise. They, very quietly, put their bags down and sat on their bed.

All too soon, the door opened, and Mike stepped out into the room. He stood with a towel around his shoulders and head; he wore no shirt, just his jeans, and was vigorously drying his hair. The instant I knew my husband had seen me, I became engulfed with a feeling of power, something I hadn't expected. I'd found him, spoilt his plans and now, he was going to do exactly what I wanted. He should have known better than to try and separate a mother from her children.

"H-hello, Julia." His voice was barely audible, looking shocked, colour draining visibly from his face.

"I thought I would come and join you for the last day of the holiday – it is the last day, isn't it?" I said innocently, my tone making it very clear that I wouldn't be going anywhere without what I came for. My eyes told him exactly what he needed to know – my children would be coming home, with or without him.

"Err, yes, yes, it's… Great. Erm, glad you, uh, glad you could come." He was sweating, words stilted, he could hardly finish his sentence.

I watched him, silently. I was in no hurry. I knew Mike must be frantically wondering how much I knew; roles reversed, it was his turn to panic. Anger rose and I had to stop myself from leaping forward, wanting to howl and scratch his eyes out. I had never felt such violence; I wanted to rage, ruin him, leave lasting scars that would serve as a reminder of how much I hated him. I had no love for him at all.

I recalled friends saying that it was impossible not to love someone, even if only a tiny bit, after separating from them, especially if the relationship had been sustained for some time. I knew, now, that wasn't true. At least, not for me. My marriage had lasted fifteen years, and I had known and loved Mike for longer than that – yet, any love I once felt: ashes. I wondered if, with time, there would ever be a reminder of what I had once felt, a ghost of a whisper. I doubted it.

"Come on, Daddy, hurry up and get dressed, we're starving. Can we go to the Sizzler for lunch? It's great there, they have a huge salad bar." Alice and Phoebe turned towards me as they described the restaurant. I played along, acting enthralled by their revelations.

"Y-yes, yes, of course. I'll be two ticks." Mike was clearly still shaken, and I was pleased to note the slight tremble of his hands as he finished drying his hair and returned to the bathroom. I hoped he was standing in front of the mirror wondering what to do next, suffering just as I had. There was no reason to rush a single moment, I wanted to prolong his agony. He had obviously not made any contingency plans for this. Eventually, he re-emerged with a white t-shirt on and slipped his feet into trainers. I noted with pleasure that his hands continued to shake.

I could feel Alice and Phoebe's eyes on me and Mike, looking at our strained faces, before they exchanged a tremulous glance with each other. I imagined they couldn't quite work out why there was so much tension in the room.

"Right, let's go then," muttered Mike, addressing us all. The twins led the way before they slowed down, linking arms with me. Feeling a wave of warmth spread through my body, I couldn't help but smile. Nobody would ever separate me from my children again. We ambled across the car park towards the Sizzler, the walk familiar to me now.

We had to wait in line to place our main course order. Alice and Phoebe were chatting loudly to each other, Mike was staring out of the window, and I watched him. I felt anger, hatred towards him, but the overpowering emotion now, was pity. I pitied him because he had sacrificed everything, and for what? Eventually, orders were taken and the four of us were shown to our table. Alice and Phoebe immediately rushed to the salad bar, leaving Mike and I alone. I took my cue.

"Why did you do it, Mike?" I whispered in a controlled voice, not wanting to attract attention knowing I had to use what little time was left. He was, again, staring out the window, looking out onto the busy Drive. He didn't answer immediately, and I wondered for a moment if he had heard me.

"You mean, you don't know?" The words were said with such venom that I was startled. Turning towards me, he looked me in the eye. "Your expensive holidays, your new cars, your shopping trips. You think all those things don't cost money? Julia, you haven't given a thought to where the money has come from for the last fifteen years. It became the only thing that ever meant anything to you, your possessions. *I* was making the money, me, not you." He spat the words out bitterly. "You didn't do a thing, not a damn thing. Then, when the girls came along, it was all about their possessions, they had to have everything – everybody was enjoying my money, except me. If I was going to get more, it was going to be mine – not yours, not anybody else's, *mine*. I didn't care where it came from, who I ripped off. I wanted money for myself and I didn't realise how damn easy it was. Then, well, there was no turning back, the decision was almost made for me. So, I was going to disappear."

The whole story sounded pathetic. He was like a child who had been caught with his hand in the sweetie jar. He had become greedy, got stupid and had been caught out. I looked at the hardness of his face and anger erupted within me. I quickly checked what the girls were doing, who had seemed to have met a friend at the salad bar and were deep in conversation.

"You listen to me, you bastard. You sell our house from under me, you take my children, you steal thousands from your own damn business, ruining not only your own life, but Alex's, your best friend – all for what? To make yourself feel like a man? You disgust me. Do you even have any idea what you've done? To me, to our daughters, to Alex? You ripped apart his business, his marriage, his *life* – he committed suicide, Mike.' I stopped, my chest heaving with ragged breaths. Mike's face was ashen as he absorbed what was being said to him. Viciously, I went on, voice low. "Oh, don't you know? Marcia ran off back to her parents as soon as Inland Revenue arrived on the scene. Alex couldn't cope and saw no other way out than to take himself off to the woods, lock himself in his car with a pipe from the exhaust and the engine running. He killed himself because of *you*.' I paused, panting, and looked up to check the girls were still occupied. They were fine, two very tanned teenage boys had their attention.

"You kidnapped my *children*. You took them to the other side of the world, hoping no doubt, that I would just lay down and die, not put up any sort of fight. Don't *ever* underestimate me again, Mike Weston. I never thought I would see the day you submitted to greed – all that crap about me and my possessions, why don't you just take a long, hard look at yourself? As for our daughters, you wanted them to have everything we never had. And where, exactly, did they fit into your great escape plan? No, Mike, you enjoyed our lifestyle just as much as any of us, you just wanted more, and more, and then you did something stupid, and got caught, so you ran away like a little boy. It's as simple as that. Don't make excuses, you pathetic, *vile* little man." There was no reply and I waited for a moment, seething.

"And just what, exactly, did you tell our solicitor? When I spoke to him after I found out – from the bloody phone company, no less – that our house was being sold, he talked to me like I was a goddamn child." I saw a flash of guilt flicker in Mike's eyes. "My god, Mike, you told him I was going mental? Perhaps a bit of a breakdown, was it? You son of a bitch, who else did you inflict your lies on?" Again, there was no answer as he stared blankly at the table, his head bowed.

The twins were making their way back to the table and as they sat down, plates piled high, I guessed it was probably the story Mike had fed most people. Suddenly embarrassed, I wondered if this was why the housekeeper, nanny and gardener had all disappeared without a trace – Mike could have told them all sorts of rubbish over weeks, or even months, prior to him disappearing.

I quietly went to the bathroom, feeling the need to freshen up and calm down. On my way back, I picked up a small plate of salad at the bar, hoping it would give me a distraction. Whilst in the ladies, I had rewound the conversation with Mike in my head. He'd tried to pin everything he'd done on me and then even the girls. What a sad, pathetic creature he had turned into. It was difficult with Alice and Phoebe around, but there was no way I was going to let them out of my sight. Mike still hadn't answered my question regarding our daughters – why had he taken them?

I knew our children meant the world to him, and he wouldn't have wanted to be without them. It was quite likely he didn't want to risk them seeing the devastation he had left in his wake, and taking them on holiday was probably the first stage of a long string of journeys. Not for the first time, I wondered if there had been another woman involved, but admitted I would never know and, more importantly, no longer cared.

I returned to the table, which I noticed was still silent; even Alice and Phoebe were whispering to each other, having picked up on the tension. As I sat down, Mike stood and went to get some salad.

As soon as he was out of ear shot, Alice asked, "What's up Mummy, you and Daddy had a row?"

"Yes, we have, darling, but don't you worry about it, love." I smiled reassuringly. I knew there was no point lying to the girls – they were thirteen, no longer babies. They may not always act as grown up as some of the teenagers I had seen around recently, but they certainly weren't stupid, and were more perceptive than even I gave them credit for, sometimes.

The twins' chatter picked up again and the main courses arrived. Mike ate in silence whilst my daughters and I continued to catch up. Dessert was another a self-service affair, which the girls loved, giggling as they left us alone again. Nervously, I steeled myself. I knew now was the time to tell Mike what was going to happen next.

"Mike, I'm taking the girls home with me tomorrow. You can do what you like. Inland Revenue, and probably the Fraud Squad, will be waiting for you if you return to England. I don't know where you stashed the money, nor do I want to. I want you to avoid contact with the girls, at least by phone, for as long as needed and I want you to stay out of our lives as much as possible. You forfeited your rights to them the moment you took them away from me. Do this, and I won't say a word to the police, or anyone else. All I'll tell them is that I managed to track you down, and you wouldn't tell me anything about the business, to protect me, and that you said you were going to come home." I paused, feeling sick to my stomach at the depth of the lie I was prepared to participate in to protect my children. I was desperate to get this part over with quickly.

"I'll also say we got to the airport and you said you had some clients to see whilst in America, and would return after you'd completed your appointments. That will be the last time I saw you." Mike made no comment, so I continued. "Mike, that is exactly what you are going to do: disappear. I don't care if you stay in America, or if you return to England, I really don't. You could go to the moon as far as I'm concerned. What we do have to do, however, is protect our children as much as we can. I think it's fair to say we will be getting divorced."

Mike's face wore a look of astonishment. I had never felt so in control, so empowered, and I wasn't sure how long it would last. I continued, "I think we should tell the twins the same story. Hold off that awful moment when they have to find out. I can then take them home in a reasonable state of mind. It's going to be hard enough for them as it is when they get home. Unfortunately, your little scam has already become public knowledge, so they're going to have to face it at some point. If you agree to this, which you better, I won't tell them how you deceived me and will try to preserve, as much as I can, their feelings for you, though god knows why." Finished now, I was exhausted. Mike still hadn't uttered a word.

Alice and Phoebe returned with their ice creams covered with at least four different kinds of sweets and smothered in butterscotch sauce. The concoction looked awful, but they ate with relish before we finally headed back to the hotel. Alice and Phoebe wanted to return to the pool for a while; I wasn't happy about them going somewhere without me, but relented, knowing I needed to project as normal a scene as possible.

Mike appeared to have ditched all parental participation and hadn't said a word for almost three hours. I felt a small amount of sympathy for him, though I had no reason to. Alice and Phoebe didn't seem to be upset by our lack of communication, instead, they just changed and disappeared, towels tucked under their arms.

Mike sat on one bed, I on the other. After a few moments of silence, Mike turned to me.

"I need some time alone," and with that, he stood and left.

I took the opportunity to go and see if I could find Tilly. I wanted to let her know that I had reunited with my girls. I didn't think Mike would try and take the children again; he wouldn't be able to convince them a second time. Leaving a note for Alice and Phoebe should they return before me, I closed the door to room 271.

20.

The bar was quiet. At first, it looked like there was nobody about, so I pulled up a stool and ordered a dry white wine. I didn't notice the person who sat down next to me, being lost in my own thoughts.

"Hello, little one." His voice was like a gentle caress. Turning, I smiled at Paul. He looked tired and I was instantly concerned.

"I didn't expect to see you today," I whispered, wondering if Paul could hear how loud my heart was beating.

"You almost didn't. I'm due out on the next flight to Arizona in three hours. I just happened to walk past the doorway and saw a lone drunk, a beautiful woman, no less," he teased.

"The way things are going, I actually will be a drunk before long," I replied, smiling wryly.

"That bad, honey? It'll get better, little one, I promise. I hear you have your daughters back," he said, obviously thinking he should turn the conversation to a more positive note.

"How did you know?"

"Tilly, who else? She saw the three of you earlier and came to tell me. I didn't sleep all night worrying about you. I love you, Julia, and I'm not going to let you down."

I wanted to believe him, I really did, but right now, I didn't feel I could totally trust anybody, least of all another man.

As if sensing my thoughts, I could see Paul nod determinedly to himself, before leaning across and placing a short, sweet kiss on my lips.

"I understand, don't worry. I'll just have to show you how much I care about you instead," he said, smiling softly. "You still have those phone numbers I gave you?" I nodded, enjoying the feeling of being so close to him. I wanted so desperately for him to be genuine, someone I could rely on. I was so tired of only having myself. I was amazed at how safe he made me feel. His scent drove me wild, a fresh onslaught on the senses with every encounter. I looked into his eyes and, with my own, begged to be kissed again.

His response was a kiss so deep and passionate, I felt drugged. A hazy mesh of lust and devotion fused in such a way, one couldn't be separated from the other. The kiss signalled his departure. Holding me close, he whispered he had to go. Picking up his single bag, I walked with him to the lobby. Paul told me Tilly would probably be in the coffee shop by now.

I found Tilly talking to an elderly couple. Tilly was so bubbly that I was sure one day she would just boil over – never had I seen her in any mood other than happy, or positive.

Tilly, seeing me, waved me over. After a short conversation, the elderly couple excused themselves.

"So, how did it go?"

"As well as it could have, I guess. It's wonderful though, to be back with Alice and Phoebe. They know there's something not quite right but I think they're taking it in their stride. I haven't given them any details yet – there's plenty of time for that later. We went shopping together this morning and I felt so happy I could have burst! It was as if we were never apart. Of course, then I had to deal with their father and almost became homicidal." I went on to describe the confrontation in detail.

"God, it sounds awful. What do you think Mike will do?"

"I don't know, I really don't. I'm hoping he goes along with my plan. If not, the only option is to go to the police, explain that I think my children are in danger and have him arrested. It would be extreme, but at least it would give me some time to get the girls and me on a plane home."

"You'd do that?" Tilly sounded impressed at my audacity.

"In a heartbeat." My voice was cold and gave no room for doubt. "I don't think Mike will try and take the girls away from me again. I know too much and he needs time to think, to work things out."

"Will you tell them the truth?" asked Tilly, as if doubting it were possible to keep it from them.

"I'll have to, I'm sure, at some point. For now, though, it's best they think Mike and I are just fighting., and I want to keep it that way until we're home. I told Mike that if he agreed to let us go, I'd keep the more, erm, unsavoury, aspects of his actions from them for as long as possible. God knows why, the bastard certainly doesn't deserve it." I could feel myself getting riled up again just thinking about what I had gone through – and no doubt would continue to go through, for some time to come. Diverting my thoughts, I checked my watch.

"I better get back. The girls probably look like a pair of lobsters by now, claiming cruelty by their mother for not having eaten in the last thirty minutes." I smiled as I said this, never wanting to forget the joy I felt every time I thought of my daughters.

"Give them my love, I've missed them today. They made my job easy," Tilly smiled.

"I'll tell them." I turned while walking away and mouthed my thanks silently, before waving goodbye.

Tilly responded in kind, grinning.

***

Finding the girls still at the pool, relief flooded through me like a tidal wave. I wondered for how long this would continue to happen – what damage had Mike done? The pair waved as I approached.

"Hi, *Mom*." I laughed at Phoebe's attempt to sound American.

"You and Daddy patch things up yet?" Alice asked, pointedly.

"No, I'm afraid not." I couldn't lie.

"Are you going to get divorced?"

I didn't answer straight away, being shocked they had even been thinking about such things, but I knew that if they had, they'd probably be prepared to accept it, in time.

"I don't know what will happen, but I want you both to understand that your father and I love you very much, no matter what happens between the two of us." I put my arms around them both. Phoebe looked as if she might cry, but no tears fell. The three of us sat in the warm sunshine, hugging. I knew I would never tire of feeling them close to me. I gently kissed both foreheads, before standing.

We went back to room 271, the girls saying they wanted to get changed. While they were busy, I collected my own bags from my room, deciding not to hand the keys back until the following day. When I returned, there was still no sign of Mike, but it was obvious my daughters had been discussing us. Phoebe's eyes looked red from crying, but Alice was her usual self.

"Right then, what would my darling daughters like to do next?" I tried to sound as bright as possible. From all the acting I'd been doing lately, I could probably warrant an Oscar nomination.

"Could we go to the outlet mall at the other end of the Drive?"

"We could catch a bus, there's one every fifteen minutes or so," Alice suggested. I guessed they had researched this quite well, knowing Mike wouldn't have let them go on their own.

"We still have a few dollars to spend," Phoebe added, obviously feeling better.

"I suppose we could, I haven't seen this mall. Yes, let's go then." I was happy for the distraction.

On the bus, Phoebe asked where her father was, and I truthfully answered that I didn't know. I also told them both about his business meetings in America and that he may go straight to them instead of coming home with us. I did this with my fingers crossed, hoping they would forgive me when the time came. It seemed to be well received; I surmised they were used to their father going away on business.

The shopping trip to the mall was a great success, though we didn't really buy a great deal. Some earrings, a lipstick, a new baseball cap – just little things that used up the last few notes and coins. I was a little alarmed when we emerged from the shopping complex, it was getting dark and we were in an unfamiliar part of town. I needn't have worried; a bus drew up as we neared the curbside, and we headed back to the hotel.

In no time, we were safely ensconced in their room, eating burgers and fries from a fast food place and choosing a pay-per-view movie. The hotel provided an excellent movie library with all the latest releases to choose from – all the more attractive due to America often having blockbusters released much sooner than England. Of course, it had its downsides – the choice was so vast that Alice and Phoebe had been bickering for forty-five minutes and still hadn't made a final choice.

I eventually chose one for us and we settled down to watch, snuggled under the covers of the bed my children had shared. I'd decided on sharing their bed with them that night. They, fortunately, had been thrilled at the idea. Mike still hadn't returned and I tried to allay their fears with false explanations of meetings, explaining he may have gone downtown to use the business facilities there.

***

In reality, it appeared Mike had found solace in the bottom of a bottle, if his stumbling through the door in the early hours of the morning was anything to go by. I'd been awoken by the sound of him vomiting on the carpet next to his bed. Sighing, I cleaned up the mess and put him to bed as best I could, grateful that neither of the girls appeared to have heard him.

I didn't sleep anymore that night, my mind spinning. I wasn't happy telling lies to the children, but wanted to get them home before the truth had to be faced; their life was going to be difficult enough, and I vowed that until then, I would try and keep things as happy as possible.

The more I thought of our situation, the more I felt overwhelmed by sadness. Even now, I naïvely wished everything could go back to how it was before – I wanted to wake up in my bed at home and for this all to have been a bad dream. Logically, I knew I wasn't the same person of a few days ago and, if I were being honest, I didn't want to be that person again – but I hated the man in the bed next to me for what he had destroyed.

I knew I had played my part though – I hadn't paid enough attention to what was going on around me. I should have been more careful, less reliant on others. There was also a guilty grain of truth in what Mike had said, possessions had become too important to me, and I hadn't fully appreciated Mike, or his needs. Of course, none of this excused his actions, and I wasn't accountable for him doing what he'd done, or becoming the person he now was.

Snuggling up to my daughters, I was thankful I hadn't been made to pay the ultimate price – I still had my children and for that, I was eternally grateful.

***

The twins woke early the next morning, surprisingly excited at the prospect of going home. I, on the other hand, was full of apprehension and dread. I knew that within twenty-four hours, our lives would irrevocably change, and having already experienced the fear that came with having your world turned upside down, I was better prepared than they. Alice and Phoebe were used to luxury, wanting for nothing – this trip to America was a normal occurrence to them, just the most recent holiday in a very long list.

They were expecting to return to their own home, their own rooms and for everything to be normal. I couldn't even guarantee they would still have their old friends; as experience had taught me, there are very few real friends that stick around when things go wrong. Instead, we'd be returning to a single car stuffed to the brim with as many saleable items as could be crammed into the boot – assuming, of course, that it hadn't been taken by now along with everything else. I sent up a silent prayer that that wasn't the case. I'd managed to pack a few of the girls' things, but nothing more than school uniforms and winter coats.

I had decided we would stay in a bed and breakfast initially. On Monday, Alice and Phoebe could return to school. There was a little comfort in the knowledge that they would be boarding, something that wasn't new to them and hopefully wouldn't object to. I would then have to find a job and somewhere more permanent to stay. My tears mixed with the warm shower water, having sought the solace of the bathroom as soon as I had woken.

I emerged to find my daughters frantically packing, jabbering away to each other noisily. Mike, it appeared, had woken accompanied by a hangover. He was sitting on the edge of his bed, his head in his hands. Something snapped inside me and I curtly asked the twins to go to reception and check the time of the coach to the airport. They were taken aback by my tone, but knew better than to argue. I closed the door behind them and turned to my husband.

"Now, you listen to me, Mike Weston. I'm doing my utmost to keep as normal a picture as possible for our children's sake until we leave here. I then have to attempt to rebuild our lives. They have no idea what you've done, but they will by this time tomorrow. So, I suggest you buck up and bloody well do the same!" I almost spat the words I was so angry. I took a breath to calm myself, but my temper flared again when Mike lifted his head and looked at me, eyes full of self-pity.

"Jesus, Mike, you're to blame for most of this! Take some damn responsibility and at least try to keep our daughters happy until tomorrow." To be honest, I knew that I would have to tell them the truth during the flight home, if not before.

Mike looked at me and a single tear fell down his face. My anger fled, leaving only exhaustion in its wake.

"I'm sorry." His words were barely audible.

"I'm sorry too, Mike, but we have to stop thinking of ourselves. We have our children to consider."

"What are you going to do? When you get home, I mean."

"Start over. I've arranged boarding for the girls, but I'll have to find us somewhere to live and get a job." I was surprised at how confident I sounded.

"What, you? What can you do?" There was more than a hint of scorn in his tone, but I didn't react.

"You'd be surprised," was all I answered. "I suggest you get yourself showered and straightened out before Alice and Phoebe return." As he got up and walked towards the bathroom, I had to ask; "Mike, what would you have done if I hadn't found you?"

He paused for a moment.

"I don't really know. I thought maybe I could create a new life for me and the girls somewhere." Looking like he was going to say more but decided against it, Mike turned away. Just before he closed the bathroom door, he turned back. "I do love our children, Julia." He stared blankly, eyes unfocused.

"You have a strange way of showing it." I had a horrible feeling that, had I not found them, Mike would never have come back to England. I felt sure that, eventually, he would have told the girls I had succumbed to whatever imaginary illness it was that had allegedly plagued me. And that would have been the end of my story, at least in my children's eyes.

***

The remainder of the morning was spent in the coffee shop, watching the twins saying goodbye to their new-found friends. Tilly stopped by and I gave her a gold chain, bought the previous day as a thank you gift. It had been relatively expensive, though only a fraction of what I knew I owed my friend. Tilly checked I still had her mobile number and also gave me the number of her mother.

I couldn't give an address, not knowing myself where we were going to live, but I did give her the number of Mike's mobile, warning her that it may now be disconnected. I felt better having been able to provide at least something in return. Tilly was also privy to the address of the school Alice and Phoebe attended – this I thought of as an insurance policy, in case anything happened to either me or Mike, knowing I could no longer rely on their godmother, Marcia.

We chatted for a while about various mundane topics: the forthcoming flight, what the weather was like in England – neither of us wanted to touch on painful subjects. Mike made an appearance just after lunch, joining the twins as they chatted to their friends. It galled me to think he'd enjoyed the intimacy of getting to know our daughters' new acquaintances.

After a while, he came over to say he would be happy to drive us to the airport. He also informed me that he had told Alice and Phoebe that he would be going on a couple business trips straight from Orlando, so wouldn't be returning home with us.

"Have you told them anything else?" I asked bitterly, amazed by his flippant attitude. "Have you told them about how you sold their home, or that their godfather took his own life?" Mike didn't answer, and I was angry at myself for the outburst. I'd asked him to act normal, and he had – there was no reason for it to annoy me.

"I'll be back in an hour to pick the three of you up," he said finally, as if he hadn't heard what I had said.

I returned to the bar, feeling I had adequate cause under the circumstances. Nursing a drink, straight vodka, I was grateful there were few people around. Tension was beginning to build inside me, forming knots at the base of my neck which I tried in vain to alleviate, knowing if I was this tense now, I'd be stiff as a board by the time I boarded the plane. The eight-hour journey would already be bad enough, and I didn't need any further inflictions.

Time ticked by far too fast and, eventually, I rounded up the twins, sitting in the lobby as we waited for Mike before he arrived, as promised. Then, as if from nowhere, Tilly also appeared. She hugged the twins and thanked them for their help, offering them a job when they were old enough – both excitedly agreed this would be excellent as they squeezed onto the back seat of the car, surrounding themselves with their belongings.

The girls and Mike looked on, a little puzzled, as Tilly and I hugged, our affection obvious as we both wiped away tears. I was unable to speak, emotions running high. Before long, we were pulling out of the car park and heading towards the airport. I expected questions from my husband, or even my children, asking about Tilly but none came, all their attention seemingly channelled elsewhere.

I found myself relieved, reticent to share details of my relationship with Tilly. There was an undeniable, deep-seated need on my part to keep as much secret from my husband as possible – the less he knew, the less he could use against me. When the girls were a little more settled, I'd tell them about Tilly and the role she played in reuniting our family, and how I would be eternally grateful to her for that.

The journey to the airport wasn't a long one. I selfishly wished it had taken more time, keen to put off the inevitable. Mike's driving was erratic; twice he had drifted into adjacent lanes of traffic, sounds of horns blaring as angry motorists made their feelings clear. My nerves, already on edge, were in tatters by the time we reached the terminal building. Driving to the underground rental car park, Mike explained to the attendant that he was only dropping off family which allowed him to park in a temporary bay in the drop-off area. I removed our bags from the boot and sent the twins to get a trolley. There was silence between us as we waited for our daughters to return, nothing more to be said.

At the airport check-in, Alice, Phoebe and I handed over our bags and tickets. The airport was sunny inside and a comfortable temperature, and I was surprised to find myself feeling a little more relaxed. Mike said goodbye to our children as he would any other time he was due to go away on business and I couldn't watch, tears stinging my eyes, as the girls reminded their father not to forget their customary gifts. The pain I was feeling, acute in its intensity, was on their behalf, not wanting to think about what lay ahead for them.

Mike and I performed a perfunctory goodbye and the three of us stood, mute, as we watched Mike disappear into the crowds. I thought parting from my husband would have been more painful and felt a perverse, momentary twinge of pride that it wasn't.

"Okay, who's hungry?" It was the only thing I could think of that would guarantee a positive response.

A bit later on, as I was sipping my tepid coffee in McDonald's, I watched my children, knowing now was as good time as any to start preparing them for what was to come.

"Girls, I have some things I need to discuss with you." I said it as gently as possible, knowing what I was about to say would change their lives forever. "When we get home, we're going to have to stay in a bed and breakfast for a time." Alice and Phoebe looked totally bewildered and I continued, "Daddy has made some bad decisions and has had some problems with the business, so he had to sell the house. I'm going to get a job though, so don't worry, we're going to be fine," I added, trying to sound enthusiastic. "You'll go to school, just like normal, but you're going to be boarding, at least for a little while. I think it's only fair that I tell you we don't have the sort of money we used to, so we're going to have to cut back on our spending." It was no good, I couldn't make it sound better than it was. I didn't want to lie to them more than I had to; they'd had enough of those. In some respects, I wished they were still toddlers, instead of teenagers. I wouldn't have to explain why their life was changing so much, and they would be young enough to adjust without too many problems, not remembering the lifestyle they used to have. This, though, would be so devastating for them that it hurt it to think about.

"Are we completely broke?" asked Phoebe.

"Yes, sweetheart, pretty much," I replied, watching their faces and waiting for the inevitable questions.

"How did Daddy lose all our money?" asked Alice.

"He took money that should have been left for the tax man. The tax man found out and froze the whole business, as well as everyone's bank accounts."

"Is that why Daddy didn't come home with us?" Alice probed again.

"Partly, yes." I spoke softly, feeling the need to be gentle. "I'm afraid the papers printed the story while you were away. You may find people will try to talk to you about it and I'm sure you'll come across some people who'll be quite nasty at times, possibly even at school. There's the likelihood you'll find out who your real friends are, those that will stick by you. At some point though, this will all fade away and people will lose interest, but it's going to take time." I waited for a reaction. The girls continued to slurp their drinks, picking at the remainders of their meals.

"What about you, Mum, what will happen to you?" Phoebe floored me with her question, bringing tears to my eyes. Both children, crying now, left their seats to hug me, making me weep all the more.

"I'll be fine, just as long as you two are," I eventually said.

"We'll be all right," Alice replied. "We have each other, and you have both of us, so we'll all be fine." I was amazed at Alice's positive outlook, humbled.

"I hate Daddy," Phoebe blurted out.

"No, you don't, not really." I knew they'd react like this at some point. I also knew that, eventually, they'd lay the blame at my feet. I wasn't looking forward to that time and hoped it would be fleeting, a backlash of anger that just needed venting.

With all three of us acutely aware of our financial situation, we took a short walk around the duty-free shops, indulging only in window shopping before drifting towards the departure lounge. It broke my heart to have to deny my daughters anything, something I'd never had to do before.

The departure lounge was almost full when we arrived, but we found three seats to the rear of the section designated for our flight, none of us wanting to be sociable with other passengers. I sat in the middle with an arm around each of my daughters, feeling closer to them than ever. Allowing myself a tiny amount of relaxation, I decided to try and get some sleep. I closed my eyes, letting my head fall back slightly and rest on the back of the chair, content in the knowledge I had my children and we were going home.

21.

I thought I was dreaming. I heard laughter and, no longer sensing my daughters at my side, I panicked, a cold sweat spreading over me. Opening my eyes, momentarily unable to focus, I saw a familiar face.

"Tilly, what on earth are you doing here?" I gasped, trying to calm my racing heart, before smiling.

"Some greeting that is! I'm due some holiday, so thought I might invite myself along and come stay in England for a while." She laughed, her attempts at nonchalance failing miserably. I felt a surge of appreciation before my heart plummeted, face falling as I remembered we had nowhere to live, let alone somewhere with room for a guest.

Tilly read the expression and placed her hand in her jeans pocket, producing a key with an Oscar-winning flourish. For a moment, I stared blankly, thinking Tilly was trying to tell me I'd forgotten to hand in my room key at the hotel.

"This, my dear, is the key to a friend's house and I have it for as long as I like, or should I say, *we* have it for as long as we like. That is, of course, if you don't mind a roomie?"

I laughed, unable to believe my luck. "We would love a roomie! But, wouldn't your friend mind me and my brood crashing there?" I questioned, a look of concern crossing my face. The twins were overjoyed with Tilly's sudden appearance and begged me to let us stay with her friend.

"There's absolutely no problem with you all staying with me. Like I said, as long as you can put up with my dreadful habits."

We were all laughing now.

The flight was called and all four of us boarded. Somehow, Tilly had managed to get a seat next to us and I was, again, amazed by my friend's resourcefulness. The journey back to England flew by and before long, we were madly grabbing our luggage from the carousels and making our way out of the airport.

Once out of the airport, we began looking for my car. I could only remember that I'd left it in the middle, somewhere. There was mild panic beginning to spread through me as I thought the worst; maybe the car had been seized, after all everything else I'd owned had. Half an hour later it was spotted by Phoebe. Having forgotten just how much I'd managed to cram into the boot, the twins ended up sitting on their cases with mine and Tilly's balanced on their laps. None of this seemed to matter though, as an almost carnival atmosphere ensued and, for now, every problem seemed almost comic – particularly when Alice pointed out that I had actually packed two left shoes for her to wear to school.

The address for the house Tilly had been able to acquire was about an hour away from the twin's school. The girls now, of course, didn't want to board, not wanting to miss out on any of the fun while Tilly was around. Fortunately, Tilly managed to talk them into staying at school during the week and coming home at the weekends – another reason to be grateful for Tilly I noted, as I made an imaginary list of all the things she'd done for me and my family.

As we drew up to the house, I was amazed. It was an old farmhouse on the outskirts of a small village. The front of the house was covered in wisteria, huge garlands of the purple flowers hanging around the windows and door frames. There was a large garden that encompassed the property on three sides and the front had a long fence running the full length of the property. It was beautiful – even Tilly was speechless, apparently not having expected such grandeur.

"Who did you say owned this place?" I said as I stared in awe.

"An old school friend who's off travelling the world," Tilly replied, before running off with Alice and Phoebe to explore. I got the feeling she was hiding something but was too grateful to push any further.

The house had obviously been prepared for our, or at least Tilly's, arrival. There was a lovely old walk-in larder, fully stocked, and the fridge was overflowing with an abundance of food, looking as though farmer's market had set up shop. There were four large bedrooms and one smaller guest room. All the beds had been made and there were antique rugs scattered over the old oak floorboards. Alice and Phoebe ran through the upper floor, bickering good-naturedly over who would get what room. They chose separate rooms, but I knew they would almost always end up sleeping together in one room or the other. I was pleased to see them so happy with their new living arrangement and offered up a silent prayer of thanks.

After emptying the car, even I had to laugh at the obscure collection of items I had deemed worthy of being kept. I could only surmise that I had been somewhat frantic at the time but was sure they would prove useful at some point, unlike Phoebe's two left shoes. As soon as we had all had something to eat, the girls decided to take a bath which I knew was their secret code for wanting to talk to each other in private. I didn't mind; they needed to work things out for themselves and it was good they had each other to speak to.

I sat down with Tilly and explained what my financial situation was, in detail. I had very little money but wanted to help pay towards the rent. Tilly told me there was no rent to be paid – the house was on loan from a friend. All that had to be settled was the electricity bill, when it came. Had it been any one else I would have been suspicious, but it was Tilly and I trusted her implicitly.

I rang the school and told a delighted Mrs Anderson that the children would be returning to school on Monday, providing jetlag didn't hit them too hard. Tentatively, Mrs Anderson asked after their father. I answered in a short, but polite manner, explaining that he hadn't returned with the family. I also thanked her for the offer of the position of caretaker but had decided against it.

I thought it might not be such a good idea to be around Alice and Phoebe too much; they needed to re-establish themselves in light of recent events. It might also give extra ammunition to some of the more unscrupulous characters they were likely to come up against, both in school and out. The headmistress said she understood entirely, adding that would keep an eye out for the children. I thanked her once more for all her help.

The drunken feeling of jetlag was beginning set in, and I decided to take a nap. Tilly had already gone to her room, quite used to dropping everything and grabbing her sleep when she could get it. On my way to my room I checked in on the girls, who were still in the bathroom. One was in the bath, the other sitting on the floor, painting her toes with her back against the bath. A regular ritual that I'd witnessed numerous times before.

The cotton bedspread felt decadent against my skin and I was asleep within minutes. When I woke up, it was dark outside, and the house was silent. Again, I felt a rise of panic, halfway down the stairs before I heard voices. Calming, my heart resumed its normal beat and the hairs on the back of my neck relaxed as I leisurely made my way towards the noise. The kitchen was filled with the smell of casserole, baked potatoes and vegetables. Tilly had an apron on, and the girls had obviously had a flour fight, now in the middle of cleaning up.

"Is there anything you can't turn your hand to?" I asked, smiling at my friend and feeling guilty for not having helped.

"One Cordon Bleu cookery course, or at least two weeks of a six-week course, and I'm Delia Smith," she laughed, wiping her hands on her apron. We ate until we were comfortably full and then toasted marshmallows on the open, woodburning fire in the living room, which I'd surprised myself in getting to light first time.

The twins said goodnight to us both and went to bed. I was grateful they hadn't questioned mine and Tilly's relationship too much yet — it would happen eventually, I knew, but hopefully I'd be better equipped to deal with answers by then. Tilly and I sat contentedly, chatting.

"How were they when you told them what had happened?"

"I haven't told them everything yet. I told them we've lost the house, and when they asked how, I said their father had taken money that belonged to the tax man, and the authorities found out and shut down the business. Mike and I agreed on an explanation as to why he didn't return home with us, but I think they suspect the real reason. They also know that there's a strong possibility that Mike and I will be getting divorced." My voice was clipped, and each sentence delivered as if read from an autocue. Now that I was saying the details out loud, it hit me how absurd this all was.

"They don't know about Alex then, yet?"

"No, I didn't want to tell them everything all at once. I found it devastating, I can't even imagine how they'll take it… he was their godfather, they loved him.' Staring into the dancing yellow-orange flames, I ran over the events of the last two weeks again in my mind.

"Tilly, I'm so eternally grateful to you. Not only are you an amazing friend, you've put a roof over mine and my children's heads," I said, gesturing to the room around us.

"Look, I was staying here anyway – consider it as keeping me company."

"How long are you really going to be here for?"

"I'm thinking of trying for a position here in the UK, so at least three or four months."

"They allow you that much holiday?" I was shocked.

"Only if you're trying for a transfer. I'll be expected to attend interviews and, if successful, will have to start work straight away."

"Would that mean you have to live near a specific airport?" I was worried, thinking Tilly may have to give up the house quickly.

"No, not at all. Ask any flight attendant or people who travel a lot for work and they'll tell you almost all of them live miles away from an airport. It's almost as if having to travel all the time makes you want your home as far away as possible; it becomes a retreat almost."

I relaxed a little and apologised for appearing selfish, feeling like I was on edge all the time. Tilly promised I wouldn't have to worry about somewhere to live for a long time yet. With that, we pushed the embers through the grate so the fire only gently glowed and went to bed.

***

On Sunday, we all woke late and had a lazy breakfast. We spent the rest of the day playing Scrabble and cards, rain pouring outside. Eventually, I persuaded Alice and Phoebe to get their school bags ready and told Phoebe she would have to wear one of the main pairs of shoes she had bought whilst on holiday for the time being. This meant, of course, that Alice had to be allowed to do the same.

When they finally took themselves to their rooms to get ready for school, Tilly decided to go for a walk, claiming cabin fever, and I found myself alone in the quiet living room. I thought of Paul, my heart aching. I missed him so much. I didn't know when I would hear from him, only hoping it would be soon. Shaking my head, I took myself upstairs to supervise a noisy debate between Phoebe and Alice.

Monday dawned, chilly and bright. The twins were looking forward to showing off their tan and seeing their friends again, their bags packed for the week. I drove them to the school gates as usual. Kissing both girls, telling them I loved them, we then hugged; and then they were gone, leaving me bereft. I watched the other parents and nannies to see if anybody was watching any of us, but all was normal. Perhaps we weren't such big news after all, I thought hopefully.

Getting back to the cottage, I entered just as Tilly was finishing a phone call.

"Yes, she's as fine as can be expected. I'll speak to you again tomorrow. See you, bye." Tilly hadn't seen me come in.

"Who was that?" I asked, unwinding the brightly coloured scarf I'd worn to ward off the chill.

"Oh, just my friend, the one who owns the house. He was just checking to see how I was settling in and I told him about you and that I'd invited you to stay – only that you were having a hard time, nothing specific. He said it's not a problem, don't worry," Tilly said, smiling reassuringly.

My mind was full of Paul. As soon as I'd had a spare moment, I'd thought of nothing else during the drive back to the cottage, longing for his touch, the warmth of his body.

Tilly and I discussed what I might be able to do for a living. Tilly offered to put feelers out with the tour operators for anything that may be available, ideally something office-based to start with. I checked my building society account; I still had enough money to last for some time, particularly as I didn't need to worry about rent right now.

***

After almost two weeks, life was beginning to settle down. The twins weren't having much trouble at school, nothing they couldn't handle between them anyway. Mrs Anderson had somehow worked out that I didn't need to worry about boarding fees for a couple of months, claiming there had been an accounting error that had only come to light when the figures were revisited; apparently, I had been overpaying in the past.

It was a warm day at the end of the second week back in England when I took the call. I'd been hoping it was Paul, having tried to contact him using all the numbers he'd supplied me to no avail. It hadn't been Paul. It was the police.

The officer I spoke to asked curtly if they could come and see me. I had given them my contact details when I'd returned from America, guessing this might happen. Of course I agreed, and waited anxiously for the visit.

I opened the door to the knock on the front door and greeted the police officer. Initially, I had thought the visit was about the embezzlement. What they had come to tell me, however, was far worse. They'd received notification from officers in America that Mike had been killed in a car crash. They had managed to trace him back to the area through the contents of his wallet – it had taken some time, as the address on his documents led to a property no longer owned by him.

The officer handed me the battered wallet. I felt numb, vision greying, and took the brown leather wallet, hands trembling as I placed it on the table next to me. For some reason I didn't want to hold it for too long. The officers again offered their condolences and left; their job done.

I was in shock, unable to move. I was still sitting in the same position when Tilly returned from shopping. It took a full ten minutes before I could bring myself to tell her about the visit, my emotions a mess.

When Alice and Phoebe came home from school that weekend, I had to tell them. They cried for most of the weekend and, come Monday, still weren't fit for school. I rang Mrs Anderson, explaining the situation, and she was understandably sympathetic. By Wednesday, Phoebe and Alice were strong enough to return to school.

The police visited again and explained that, in light of Mike's death, the authorities wouldn't be pursuing the case any further. Relieved, life continued, though for some time, I felt I was simply going through the motions, a dull haze surrounding me.

A couple of weeks after Mike's death, I was clearing out some of the girl's cupboards with them when I came across the large tote bag Alice always used when on holiday. The bag had a large inner pocket and as I was folding the bag, trying to fit it into one of the unused pigeonholes, I felt a small, thick packet. I called to Alice, who was just going downstairs, not wanting to go through my daughter's possessions. Alice looked confused initially, before her face took on a look of panic.

"Oh god, Mum, I'm sorry. Daddy gave me that the morning we left Florida, he asked me to give it to you when we arrived home, but I forgot. I'm so sorry, Mum." Tears streamed down her pale face.

"It's okay, sweetie, it's okay, it doesn't matter, really. Here, let's open it now." I wanted to calm her down and slowly, we opened the package. Inside was a thick wad of one hundred-dollar bills. Alice and I, with shaking hands and tears falling freely, counted ten thousand dollars in total. Mike must have known I wouldn't take any money from him, had it been offered, deeming it blood money. This was obviously why he had given it to Alice. I wouldn't have been able to return the money to him anyway, between not having had an address and my insistence that he stay away. The money was almost untraceable, having been brought from the US and the bills were noticeably used, crumpled. I had no idea how he had obtained it, no idea as to its history, nothing.

The amount was relatively nominal in comparison to the expenditure of our old lifestyle, but now, it was a fortune. Not knowing of its history and noting the serial numbers were out of sequence, I felt it would be safe to use, if done carefully. I physically felt a weight lifted from my shoulders.

There was no need to look for a job for a little while, now that we had some funds. Every now and then, I'd exchange a couple of the bills and the money would pay for food or clothes for us all.

There still had been no word from Paul. Almost three months had passed, but I still held out hope. I had made the decision, however, that if he didn't contact me soon, I would stop calling and carry on with my life. I knew I would never want another man; my life would be devoted to my children.

The wallet the police had handed to me I had eventually placed in a drawer, not wanting to be reminded of him. It was only when I decided I needed to have a clear out did I come across it again. Mike had always rammed so much into his wallet that it barely closed, and the leather was well worn and stretched. He'd rarely carried cash but had numerous cards, and always kept the receipts for everything. It was as I was sorting through the receipts that I came across the two letters.

The first one I found was in amongst the dozens of receipts. It was written on thin paper, almost like airmail paper, bright blue. It was dog-eared, as if he'd read it over and over, the folds opened and closed so many times that they looked as though they might split at any moment. I unfolded it carefully. At first, I couldn't decipher the handwriting, but after a moment of concentration I was able to follow the scrawl. My heart thudded as I read the words.

My Darling Mike,

I cannot believe after only a few weeks I feel so much love for you. I love you, my darling, and I am looking forward to our life together. I am sad to go home to America, but happy knowing it will be only a little while before you join me.

That rainy day we met, my first day at Claremont and Weston, was the best day of my life and I will treasure it always. I will wait for you, my love, and make plans for our new home, just me and you.

Hurry, my love, hurry.
Estou apaxonado
I am in love with you.
Your love,
Bea x

I felt sick. A flood of anger rose, making me want to scream and it was a second before I realised I was. I wanted to call him a lying, cheating bastard – I wanted him to *pay* for what he had done. But he had paid, hadn't he, he'd paid for everything he'd done, with his life. There was nothing I could do to make him pay any more than that, so why then did I feel so cheated?

I should have known better; I knew he hadn't been strong enough to go on with life alone. He was a coward, he had no backbone to start over without someone else – of course he would have needed someone to feed his ego, boost his entitled sense of self-worth.

My blood continued to boil, though I was as angry with myself, as much as I was with Mike, feeling foolish for having ever believed a word that came out of his lying, wretched mouth. Even in death, Mike was able to make me feel inadequate. It was impossible to tell the age of the author, but I assumed she must have been relatively young. If she were older, she would have been more literate, more refined, even if English was her second language. It was a disjointed letter, the sentences short and simple and the foreign phrase only added to my suspicions.

I read and re-read the letter, inflicting the pain on myself repeatedly. I would pace the room like a caged animal after putting the letter down, only to pick it up again. After a time, even touching the letter made me feel tainted. I folded it and placed it to one side, knowing it wouldn't be the last time I looked at it.

Needing the distraction, I continued emptying the contents of Mike's wallet. A driving licence, showing an unflattering picture, still showed our old address and I mused for the millionth time how much my life had changed in such a short space of time.

The wallet now empty, I turned it over in my hands, marvelling at how my husband, of so many years, had had his entire existence boiled down to a meagre pile of receipts and plastic. Inspecting the wallet once more, I saw the zipped edge of a pocket that ran the length of the wallet. It didn't feel like there was anything in it, but I opened it anyway. It was there that I discovered the second letter.

The envelope had been sealed, never opened, and was, again, the same thin, blue paper, together with matching envelope. I didn't know if Mike had known it was there, or if, perhaps, it had slipped his mind, having been busy putting his plans into practice.

For a fleeting moment, I felt it wasn't my place to read the unopened letter that quite obviously wasn't meant for me. Shrugging, I pushed that aside and opened the envelope carefully, the paper feeling so fine I thought it may disintegrate at any moment. Having never been read, the ink and handwriting were a little more clear, and I could tell from the start it was a different tone from the original.

Mike,

I am writing this letter to say goodbye. You will not be seeing me ever again. I am going home, not to America but to Brazil, to my true love Carla, we are to be married. She has been waiting too long for me. I tell you this as I want you to know the truth about me. As you know I come from Brazil, but what you don't know is that my family are very poor, and I left with the aim to return home one day with enough money to look after them. Now I have the money you gave me, I can go home and be happy.

You cannot be mad at me. You have lied too. You are married and you have children. You did not tell me this. You are a bad man, like all men. Do not follow me.

Goodbye Mike.

Bea

Now dumbstruck, my anger evaporated. Mike had been duped by a woman, a woman who didn't even like men. I cackled hysterically, aware I couldn't quite bring myself to stop. I felt vindicated, maybe even slightly in shock; Mike had been just as foolish as me, perhaps even more so, albeit in a different way. I had won. He had lost.

I folded the second letter and took them upstairs to my room. I didn't want Phoebe or Alice to stumble across them, though I didn't want to get rid of them just yet either, unsure why. The contents of both letters stayed with me all day, but I didn't tell Tilly. I didn't think it would serve a purpose; he was gone.

22.

Returning from a trip to the local bakers one clear, chilly morning, I let myself into the kitchen, and busied myself putting away the treats I'd picked up. Suddenly, I heard a noise. Thinking we might be being burgled, knowing no one was supposed to be home, I took a knife from the kitchen drawer. Quietly, I tiptoed to the living room. Opening the door, I saw a man with his back towards me.

At that moment, my toe caught on the companion set beside the fireplace and it fell to the floor with a loud crash. The man turned, startled, and I gasped as I recognised the face.

"Paul! Oh my god, what are you doing here?"

"Hello, little one. That was certainly an interesting greeting." His soft smile melted my heart, before hardening.

"Well, you've hardly been a regular visitor," I retorted tartly, anger rising.

"Come here." I dropped the knife as he pulled me to his chest. His scent filled my body and clouded my mind. He drew me down with him to the couch.

"Now, please listen to me and hear me out before interrupting." He planted a kiss on the end of my nose as I primly sat, quietly motioning for him to continue.

"I'm sorry I wasn't able to come here as quickly as I had hoped – my business affairs took longer than originally anticipated. So, I asked Tilly if she would accompany you all back to England. I gave her the key to my house here which, fortunately, wasn't too far away from the twins' school. As I said, things were taking their time to get sorted out.' He paused and looked into my eyes, kissing me tenderly. I could barely breathe as longing rose through my body. He continued with his story.

"I heard about your husband's death and felt it would have been inappropriate to arrive on the scene too soon – it wouldn't have helped your situation any. So, I waited. I couldn't wait any longer. Julia, I love you so much and it has been unbearable having to wait this long." He pulled me closer and kissed me hard, the pent-up passion evident. I responded in kind, the fire inside rekindling and coursing throughout my body, making me pant gently, the longing to have him nearly unbearable.

Eventually, I pulled away a little.

"So, this house is yours? All those phone calls Tilly kept getting, were you?"

"I'm afraid so. I had to swear Tilly to secrecy, so don't be mad at her – I knew you wouldn't accept any help from me directly, so I had to go behind your back. Do you hate me?"

"No, Paul, I love you. I love everything about you." I kissed him again. "How did you get Tilly to give up her job in America?"

"Oh, that was easy; she's been looking for a way to come to England for some time. I offered her this place as a way to keep an eye on you and the twins. I have to tell you; she wasn't happy about lying and was furious when I decided I would have to delay my arrival."

I heard the front door open and a minute later Tilly came into the room.

"Well, it's about time." The look of relief on her face was evident. Tilly began to apologise for having lied to me, but I wouldn't hear of it.

She turned and disappeared into the kitchen, smiling, and we suddenly heard enough noise to wake dead. I smiled to myself as I pictured my friend deliberately bashing pans together and slamming drawers as Paul led me upstairs to the bedroom.

THE END

BV - #0013 - 190421 - C0 - 197/132/15 - PB - 9781912964598 - Matt Lamination